PURITAN BRIDE

Marriage to a fugitive Royalist saves his life and gives Lucy Wetherby a home, but it also brings her face to face with a reluctant mother-in-law and the beautiful girl her husband had been meant to marry. As she tries to earn the respect and friendship of those around her, a visit from an old friend brings an unexpected stroke of good luck — but will it separate Lucy from the husband she has grown to love?

SHEILA HOLROYD

PURITAN BRIDE

Complete and Unabridged

LINFORD
Leicester

First published in Great Britain in 2003

First Linford Edition
published 2004

British Library CIP Data

Holroyd, Sheila
Puritan bride.—
Linford romanc
1. Love stories
2. Large type b
I. Title
823.9'14 [F]

ISBN 1–84395–

Holroyd, Sheila

Puritan bride /
Sheila Holroyd

ROM LP

1572246

Published by
F. A. Thorpe (Publishing)
Anstey, Leicestershire

Set by Words & Graphics Ltd.
Anstey, Leicestershire
Printed and bound in Great Britain by
T. J. International Ltd., Padstow, Cornwall

This book is printed on acid-free paper

1

Lucy Wetherby had her arms wrapped round her brother as they huddled on the floor in a corner of the room. They could hear the shouts and screams, the clash of weapons and the sound of pistols through the thick shutters fastened over the windows, which admitted only chinks of light. Thomas clung to her tightly, and she murmured comfortingly to him, trying to reassure the ten-year-old that the noise would soon end and they would be safe again.

It was two weeks since Charles Stuart had entered Worcester at the head of twelve thousand men in a desperate attempt to claim the throne of England in succession to his father, who had died on the scaffold nearly three years earlier. His small force had been exhausted after its march from Scotland and a week later, Oliver Cromwell had appeared outside Worcester with over thirty thousand soldiers, and today his men were in the city hunting down the defeated Royalists.

There was a sudden clamour nearby. Triumphant yells indicated that a group of soldiers was pursuing a victim. To Lucy it sounded like a pack of dogs closing in on their quarry for the kill. Her head lifted in alarm as something suddenly struck the door forcefully, then again. The blows were repeated. Rusty nails tore free from the wood as both the lock and the bolt yielded to the attack. The door swung open to admit a man who immediately slammed it shut and stood with his back against it, looking round the room desperately.

He did not see the two figures crouched in the darkness, but seized the heavy table that stood under the window and dragged it along until it was holding the door shut and obstructing any possible entry. Thomas whimpered in fright and the man spun round, drawing his sword from the scabbard that hung by his side.

Lucy leaped to her feet and flung herself in front of Thomas, and found the point of the sword at her throat. For a few seconds she did not breathe, and then the intruder's eyes grew accustomed to the dim light and he saw that he was threatening a young woman, with a boy clinging to her skirts.

'Don't scream!' he warned her. 'If you cry for help it will be the last sound either of you make. Do you understand, child?'

Thomas nodded dumbly, his eyes great with terror. Lucy stood upright, proudly, determined not to show her fear. For a long moment her brown eyes gazed into the hazel eyes of the man who threatened her, and then the sword point wavered and pointed down at the floor.

'Forgive me,' the man said bleakly. 'Even to save my life I will not harm a woman or child.'

At that moment, as Lucy still confronted him, the noise in the street reached their door and there was a thunderous knocking.

'Open up in the name of Parliament!' a voice demanded loudly. 'There are still a few Royalists who haven't managed to run away. Let us make sure there's none in your house!'

The intruder stood facing the door now, his sword ready in his hand, waiting for the soldiers to force the door, knowing that when they did so it would mean certain death for him. Suddenly Lucy gathered up her skirts and ran up the staircase to the first floor where she flung open the shutters and leaned out.

'Stop that noise!' she demanded shrilly as half a dozen of Cromwell's men looked up at her. 'I have a sick child here, ill with some fever. Go and hunt your prey elsewhere!'

They hesitated, murmuring to each other, and the leader looked up.

'Are you sure none of Charles Stuart's men has sneaked into your house?'

'Come and look if you must, so long as you are quiet. But you'll risk getting a fever for your pains.'

They shuffled uneasily, brave enough to face an armed man but reluctant to face an invisible threat that might bring sickness, even death.

'We'll leave you in peace to nurse the child,' the leader announced, and led his men away to another house.

Lucy pulled the shutters to once more, and rested for a moment, feeling suddenly weak and shivery. Then she made her way down the stairs with some dignity.

'You have my thanks,' the Royalist fugitive said wonderingly, 'but why did you do that?'

She shrugged. She had acted on impulse before she had thought, in fact, and now she had to rationalise her action.

'I did not want my brother to see how men kill each other,' she said.

There was silence as the two stood at a loss, and Thomas broke it.

'What do we do now?' he questioned.

'We wait till the soldiers have gone,' Lucy informed him, 'and then our unexpected guest can slip away.'

'Can we have something to eat while we are waiting? I'm hungry!' her brother complained.

This was true, and Lucy realised that she was hungry as well. They had broken their fast early that morning, but then the fighting had begun and safety had seemed more important than food. Like most town houses belonging to merchants, the ground floor of the Wetherby house was meant to be used for storing goods and as a place for trade, and the family lived in the rooms above. Lucy took her brother's hand and began to lead him up the stairs.

'I'll find us something nice,' she assured him, and then looked back at the upturned face of the man she had saved. 'I suppose you'd better come up as well,' she said grudgingly, and he followed her without a word.

With the shutters closed and the sun

already setting, the parlour was dark and unwelcoming until she had found and lit some candles. Then she felt comforted by the familiar shapes of the well-worn furniture as it emerged from the shadows. This was her home, her sanctuary, no matter what horrors were taking place outside in the streets of Worcester. She turned to the stranger, secure on her own ground.

'Stay here with Thomas,' she instructed. 'I will see what there is to eat.'

She returned ten minutes later carrying a tray with cold meat, bread and cheese, and a small jug of ale, and put it on the long, oak table before she took some pewter plates and tankards from a cupboard. It was clear that Thomas had quickly overcome any fear of the stranger for he was sitting by his side, inspecting the Royalist's pistol.

'Don't touch it!' she said urgently, but the man smiled.

'It is safe enough, mistress. I ran out of ammunition for it hours ago.'

He was eyeing the food with evident desire and she invited him to join them, feeling she could not leave a hungry man to watch them eat. He accepted with obvious eagerness, though he insisted on being shown where he could rinse his hands before he joined them.

She already knew that he was tall and brown-eyed, but by the light of the candles she could see that he had dark, well-shaped eyebrows and a determined chin, as well as shoulder-length mid-brown hair. His features were pleasant, though not especially handsome, and his manners were those of an educated man. His green coat, with a white lace collar and a red sash, might once have been a fine garment, but now it was stained and torn and the collar was dirty.

He looked up from the food he had been eating rapidly and caught her looking at him.

'I may look a ruffian now but I have seen better days,' he said ruefully. 'I am a gentleman, and my name is Martin Radford.'

She bowed her head in acknowledgement.

'And I am Lucy Wetherby, and this is my brother, Thomas.'

Martin Radford was looking round the well-proportioned parlour.

'May I take it that the rest of your family, your men-folk, are fighting on one side or the other today?'

She shook her head.

'My family has supported Parliament since the beginning of this war, but now we are all the family we have. My father died some months ago in London where he had gone on business.'

'I am sorry,' he said sympathetically, and then his voice altered and became reproachful. 'But if you two are alone in the house you should not have given me, a stranger, shelter here. I might have robbed you or done you some harm!'

Lucy gave a little snort of laughter.

'Would you rather that I had given

you up to the soldiers to kill?'

He grinned reluctantly at this.

'No. I must admit that I am grateful you acted so rashly. Once I have eaten I will leave you in peace.'

But this was easier said than done. When darkness fell the fighting seemed to intensify in the streets outside. They extinguished all but one candle and sat listening apprehensively. At one point they realised that another group of soldiers was searching the street methodically, house by house. When they knocked on Lucy's door she opened the shutters and repeated her story about the sick child, but this time they were not deterred so easily.

'We shall try not to disturb you while we search the house,' the leader told her.

She felt Martin Radford grow tense beside her. If these men came in and found him they would kill him and would know that she had been guilty of sheltering a Royalist. Quickly she stretched out her hand and pinched

Thomas viciously. Startled and hurt, he gave a scream of pain and burst into noisy sobs.

'How can you avoid disturbing him?' Lucy challenged. 'You can hear how he suffers now.'

Just at that moment, there was a shout from a short distance away. A fugitive had been found hiding in a deserted house and Cromwell's soldiers gladly abandoned Lucy's fever-ridden house in pursuit of this new prey.

'I'll go as soon as the streets are clear,' Martin Radford muttered, but once the actual fighting had died down it was replaced by the measured tramp of feet.

The Parliamentary generals had organised a watch to patrol the streets.

Lucy put Thomas to bed and went back to the parlour where the Royalist was waiting patiently.

'You'll have to stay here for the night,' Lucy said resignedly. 'You can sleep on some cushions on the settle.'

He looked exhausted and despairing,

and although he fought for the Royalists against everything she believed in, it was difficult to regard him as her enemy. She forced her tired face to smile.

'There is nothing here for you to steal, so get some rest while you can.'

He stood while she left the room, bade her good-night, and then almost collapsed on the settle.

In the morning, she found him fast asleep and stood looking down on him for some time. He looked very vulnerable. She felt pity for this young man, caught up in the bitter struggle which had torn England apart for so long. Then she must have made some movement which disturbed him, for suddenly he was awake, his hand fumbling for the sword by his side.

'There is no danger,' she told him, and he shook himself into full awareness of the slender girl who stood there.

Her hair, long and curly, was drawn neatly back under a white cap. She looked calm and composed, but there were dark shadows under her eyes.

'Thomas will be up soon. There is enough bread and cheese for breakfast.'

She went to the shutters and opened them, peering out. The street seemed empty, but as Martin Radford came to stand beside her she saw a patrol of Parliamentary foot soldiers turn the corner into the street and signed to him to keep away from the window.

Breakfast was a silent meal, soon over. Thomas was still tired, yawning and irritable. Martin Radford was obviously preoccupied with the problem of how to escape from the house and then from Worcester, and Lucy had begun to realise what a problem her impulsive action in protecting him was proving to be. Once the meal was cleared away she found a woven basket and put on her cloak.

'I must try and buy some more food, though I doubt if there will be many shopkeepers with food to sell today. At least it will give me a chance to find out what has happened in Worcester.'

She hesitated, but Martin Radford was imprisoned in her house as securely as if there were guards at the door, and she knew instinctively that Thomas was safe with him.

She was gone two hours and came back with her basket nearly empty.

'There's little trade in Worcester today, but I have a loaf at least, and some eggs.'

'What did you learn?' Radford asked, ignoring the question of food.

She frowned warningly and indicated her brother with a slight gesture.

'Thomas, will you put the eggs away carefully and then tidy your room?'

When her brother had gone reluctantly to carry out these tasks she sat down on the high-backed chair that had been her father's favourite. Martin Radford stood in front of her, scowling.

'I know it's bad news, so you need not spare me.'

She clasped her hands in her lap and gazed at him steadily.

'Charles Stuart is utterly defeated.

Cromwell himself said that the battle was as stiff a contest for four or five hours as he had ever seen, but in the end the Royalist army was completely routed.'

Martin Radford swallowed, and then spoke with a visible effort.

'I was with Charles when it looked as if we might drive the Roundheads back, but then Cromwell took charge and forced us back into Worcester. How many of our men died?'

She looked down at her clasped hands.

'It is said that some two to three thousand Royalists were killed, and many taken prisoner.'

'And the Roundheads?'

'Some say as few as two hundred.'

He sank down on the settle and buried his head in his hands.

'They were better men, led by a better commander. Our army was tired after its march from Scotland, and had lost heart. We believed that the country would welcome us and rise to support

Charles, but all we found was indifference or hostility.'

He took his hands from his face and stood upright, his hand resting on the pommel of his sword.

'All that, effort, all those lives, wasted.'

'But Charles himself has escaped! Cromwell's men have been hunting him all night but they have no trace of him so far!'

His face lit up momentarily, but then his shoulders slumped.

'So all that remains of the Stuart cause is a young man on the run from his enemies and a few dozen adherents in France surviving on the kindness of the French King.'

'He is not the only young man trying to escape his enemies. What will you do now?'

'If I can get away from Worcester I may be able to reach Derbyshire. I have an estate there where I live with my mother and sister. I think I would be safe there. I do not believe Parliament will think me worth hunting down.'

'Why did you leave it? You must have known that Charles Stuart would be defeated.'

'I am a Royalist, and we thought that we would win because right was on our side.'

He gave a rueful grin.

'Anyway, perhaps I was a little bored with being a farmer and thought it would be exciting to follow Charles.'

There was a short silence which she broke abruptly.

'This estate of yours, is it a good estate?'

'Good enough. Our farmlands are in the valley and we have a good house near a little village. My family has lived there for centuries.'

'You are not married? Are you betrothed?'

He shook his head.

'Neither married nor betrothed. It did not seem right to take on the responsibility of a family and children when the country was in turmoil.'

Her curiosity seemed to register with him at last, and he looked puzzled.

'Forgive me, but talk of my home seems irrelevant when, to face reality, it is unlikely that I shall ever see it again. After all, even if I could get away from this house and then from Worcester, I would still have a long way to go across a country which is now controlled by Parliament's men. Perhaps the best thing to do would be to walk out of here and surrender myself to some Roundhead officer. I could say that I spent the night in some outhouse.'

'You would probably be killed before you could surrender. Even if that did not happen, how many years do you think you will spend as a prisoner of war? What would happen to your estate and to your mother and sister?'

He glared at her angrily.

'What else can I do? Have you any better suggestions?'

She bent her head, veiling her eyes with her long lashes, and he turned away, annoyed at himself for losing his temper when he knew she was speaking the truth. Her voice behind him was very quiet.

'I could help you escape.'

He swung back eagerly. Her features were quietly composed, showing no emotion.

'What did you say?'

'I said I could help you escape, but there would be a price.'

He waited.

'I will help you escape, on condition that Thomas and I go with you, and that you marry me.'

2

Lucy had to bite her lip to stop herself giggling hysterically at the sight of Martin Radford's bemused face.

'What did you say?' he asked incredulously, and she repeated her offer and the conditions.

He looked round at the spacious room with its solid furniture.

'Why? Why should you want to marry me and leave all this? You have a fine house, friends, a place where you are known and respected.'

He stopped abruptly, looking at her with a sudden, startled surmise, and now she did allow herself to smile.

'No, don't flatter yourself. I have not suddenly fallen madly in love with you. If you will sit down, I can explain.'

He sat down uneasily on the edge of a chair, obviously prepared to rise and flee if she showed any other signs of madness!

'In truth, I have few friends and I do not expect this house to be mine for much longer. You say this is a fine house, but haven't you wondered where the servants are or why I could leave you here alone last night because there is nothing left to steal except a few pewter plates? My father was a prosperous merchant, but trade had suffered during the war and eight months ago he went to London with all the money he could spare to invest in some projects in the Netherlands. Then a few weeks later we heard from the clerk who went with him, Walter Thomson, that he was dead. He was found dead in his bed one morning. Apparently his heart had failed. Walter sent us news that the projects had failed and there was no money to come back to us.'

She paused as the sad loss of her parent was brought to mind again.

'My father had left me with enough

to pay our way for a few weeks but after a while I had to sell our few pieces of silver and our servants left when I could not pay their wages. Then other merchants and tradesmen began to arrive with papers which they claimed proved that my father had owed them money. I could not disprove what they said and I could not afford lawyers to investigate. A boy of ten and a nineteen-year-old girl are easy victims. My father's stock was seized to settle some bills, but I know that one or two are planning to claim the house to settle what they say are my father's debts. Then Thomas and I will be homeless and penniless.'

Martin Radford looked at her wonderingly.

'And you are prepared to marry a stranger in the hope that he can give you a home?'

She lifted her chin defiantly.

'If I only had to worry about myself it wouldn't matter. I could find work of some kind as a servant in the town or on a farm, but there is Thomas. Few people would be willing to employ me if they had to feed and accommodate him as well. I will do anything to protect him.'

She leaned forward urgently.

'You say you have farms. I have run this house for my father for three years, ever since my mother died, and I am a hard worker. I would be a good wife to you, and Thomas will soon be old enough to help as well.'

He looked at her steadily for some time and then gave a deep sigh.

'I owe my life to you, and I must repay that debt if I can. If you are willing to risk a journey of hundreds of miles through England in these troubled times, then I am prepared to make you my wife, and if we reach the safety of my home I will give you and your brother shelter there.'

She closed her eyes and relaxed thankfully, then smiled bravely.

'I promise you that you will not be sorry. Now all we have to do is tell

Thomas and plan how to leave Worcester.'

The smile became almost mischievous.

'If you are to get safely through the Roundhead army, the first thing I must do is cut your hair.'

The next morning saw Lucy and Thomas leave their home. They were dressed for travelling and took with them only what they could carry easily. A manservant with roughly-cropped hair who wore a suit of clothes obviously made for a much stouter man attended them.

'People will stare at me, not because I look like a Royalist but because I look like a figure of fun,' Martin had said rebelliously.

'A manservant would not wear a lace collar,' Lucy had pointed out. 'And these clothes are of good, hardwearing cloth, though I admit that you are slimmer than my father was. You'll just have to belt them in.'

As she turned the key in the house

door for the last time, she stood for a moment looking up at the façade.

'Hurry,' Martin murmured. 'I shan't feel easy till we are safely out of Worcester.'

'This is the only home I have ever known. Give me time to say farewell.'

She bent her head for a moment as if tears threatened, and then lifted her head bravely.

'Wait while I give my neighbour the key.'

She rapped on the door of the adjoining house and explained to the woman who appeared that she and Thomas were going to stay with an aunt at Evesham, who had sent her manservant to escort them there safely.

'Will you be kind enough to keep the key and watch over the house till we return?' she asked, and the woman agreed eagerly.

'I hope she has the courtesy to wait till we have turned the corner before she starts going through our house,' Lucy commented resignedly to Martin.

'Her husband is one of the men who claims to be a creditor of my father.'

They made their way along the streets towards the road to Evesham. She had persuaded Thomas that they were going on a great adventure and his eyes were sparkling, but Lucy's heart was beating rapidly when they approached a group of Roundhead soldiers who were stopping everyone who was trying to leave town.

When they were challenged, she repeated her story of the aunt waiting for them in Evesham. The sergeant, a middle-aged man with a worried face, looked at the trio with a frown, especially at the rather unprepossessing figure of Martin, who was hanging back a little and trying to look vacant.

'There are still fugitives in the countryside,' the sergeant told Lucy. 'It might be safer to wait a few days.'

'The arrangements are made and my aunt is waiting for us,' Lucy replied.

'Wait here,' he said abruptly and strode away.

They stood in the street, expecting him to reappear any second with armed guards to arrest them, but he came back alone.

'Here,' he said, giving Lucy a folded sheet of paper. 'This is a safe conduct signed by Cromwell himself. Show it to any soldier in our army and he will help you. But be careful how you go.'

She thanked him with genuine warmth, and soon they had left Worcester and were on the road to Evesham. They walked steadily till past noon, by which time Thomas was pleading for a rest, so they settled themselves under a beech tree and ate some of the food that Lucy had packed.

'This won't last long,' she said worriedly as she packed away the remains. 'I have a little money, but not enough to pay for food and shelter all the way to Derbyshire.'

'I have this,' Martin said, feeling in a pocket and then holding out a handful of silver.

Lucy examined the money curiously.

'I haven't seen coins like this before. Where do they come from?'

'They are Scottish coins,' he told her, and she pushed the silver away.

'If anyone sees them they will know that you came from Scotland with Charles Stuart! Get rid of them!'

'But we need money!'

'We daren't use that money. It is too dangerous.'

She was right. With an angry exclamation he hurled the useless coins into the bushes around them.

'We shall have to sleep rough,' Lucy said resignedly.

'Do you mean we shall be sleeping out in the open?' Thomas said with obvious delight.

'Wait till you've spent a night trying to sleep while the rain pours down on you,' Martin said gloomily. 'I've done it more than once in the past weeks and I haven't enjoyed it.'

It was not quite as bad as that, however. On the outskirts of Evesham, they found a run-down tavern whose owner gave them some hot food and permission to sleep on some musty hay in one of the outhouses. At least it meant that they did not have to go right into the town and be seen at any of the large inns there. Cromwell's troops were in the area and would be questioning any strangers.

They slept soundly after a tiring day, but woke stiff and sore, and it took Lucy and Martin some time to persuade Thomas that he must set out on the road again. Before they turned north towards Derbyshire, Martin insisted on fulfilling part of his undertaking to Lucy. In a small village, he found a minister who agreed reluctantly to perform the marriage service for Martin and Lucy. It was a quick affair in an empty church, with only the sexton and the minister's housekeeper as witnesses.

As they stood before the altar Lucy began to panic. What was she doing marrying this virtual stranger? She should have stayed in Worcester and tried to find some answer to her problems among familiar surroundings. She glanced uneasily at Martin as he took his place beside her in her father's old suit, his cropped head bare. Then she saw how he had done his best to arrange his clothes neatly and becomingly.

He stood tall beside her, and she observed the clear-cut profile and the determined chin. At least she was not tying herself to a weakling. Many a girl would have envied her such an upstanding husband.

As if he guessed her thoughts, Martin turned his head and smiled down at her reassuringly, and his hand found hers and held it comfortingly. For an instant she thought how pleasant it would have been if they had indeed been lovers joyfully promising to share their lives.

Instead of a wedding breakfast and festivities, Martin and Lucy thanked the minister, left him at the church door, and started out again on the long road, a bad-tempered Thomas trudging beside them. The weather was deteriorating. A farm worker busy in the fields told them that a path through some woods would save them a few miles and as the trees would shelter them from the rain they decided to take his advice. However, the woods were larger than they had expected and riddled with paths in every direction. Soon, they were hopelessly lost.

'Stay here and rest,' Martin told his companions. 'I'll go ahead and look for the right path.'

At first Lucy and Thomas were glad to rest, but the wind and rain were filling the trees with strange noises. As time passed, Lucy began to wonder what had happened to Martin. Had her new husband deserted them, leaving them to wander in the woods while he strode out for his home unencumbered? She heard a rustle in the undergrowth behind her and turned round thankfully, expecting to see Martin. Instead two men in boots and leather jerkins stood there grinning unpleasantly at them.

'Pretty enough to amuse us for an hour,' one commented, jerking his head at Lucy.

'First things first,' his companion said, and beckoned commandingly to Lucy. 'Hand over your bags, girl, and let us see what you've got in them.'

'A few clothes, nothing worth taking. Let us go without harm,' Lucy entreated, but they ignored what she said.

The first man strode forward and snatched the bag she held, producing a knife with which he cut it open. At that moment, while his hands were occupied and the other man was peering at the bag to see what was in it, Martin leaped from the trees wielding a length of broken branch and knocked the watcher unconscious as the man with the bag swung round, knife at the ready.

While he stared at Martin, however, it was Thomas, screaming furious defiance, who charged at him and hit him full in the stomach with his head. He fell to the ground, his knife flying wide, and Lucy and Thomas promptly threw themselves on him, the boy pummelling away with his small fists.

'Leave him to me!' Martin instructed, and soon the man was trussed up with his own belt, after which the unconscious man was also secured.

Martin stood laughing triumphantly, his arms round Lucy and Thomas.

'The Radford army has won its first battle! You two would make fine soldiers,' he proclaimed.

'But look what a mess he has made of our things!' Lucy lamented as she tried to gather together the scattered contents of the ripped bag.

'He owes us something for that,' Martin said firmly, and began to search his two prisoners, triumphantly collecting a handful of silver and gold coins which he transferred to his own pockets.

'What shall we do with them?' Lucy

asked nervously. 'We can't leave them here to die.'

'Their bonds won't hold for ever. They'll free themselves within the hour.'

'Then they will follow us!'

'On foot? Look at their boots, Lucy. These men are riders. If we look carefully, we should find their horses.'

They left the two men, both now cursing forcefully, and a ten-minute search located two horses tethered to a tree. Neither was in particularly good condition but they were docile enough to let Martin mount one of them while the other carried Lucy and Thomas.

'They were probably deserters from one of the armies,' Martin told Lucy. 'It dosen't matter if they were Royalists or Roundheads, such men will avoid real danger and prey on travellers. At least our journey will now be much easier thanks to them.'

That night they felt it was safe to sleep in an inn. Lucy, drifting off to sleep with Thomas cuddled in her arms while Martin lay wrapped in a blanket on the floor, realised that it was her wedding night.

Before they set out the next day, Martin tended the horses and went through the saddlebags they were carrying. He returned to the inn looking thoughtful. When they were on their way he told Lucy what he had found.

'There were fifty sovereigns in one saddlebag. I suspect that one of the men was cheating his partner and secretly accumulating his own small hoard. At least we will not have to worry about money now.'

Life on the road was now very different. They could stay in respectable inns and did not have to worry where they could get food. The horses responded to good treatment and covered the miles without trouble.

Within a few days, they were approaching Derbyshire and Lucy began to think of what lay ahead. Martin and she had got on reasonably well on the journey, knowing it was in their own best interests to collaborate, but soon they would reach their future home and there might be difficulties there.

'What are your mother and sister like?' she asked him one day. 'Will they accept me?'

'Of course,' he said firmly. 'You are my wife.'

In name only, she thought. That would be another problem to face.

'But will they like me, do you think?'

He hesitated now, brooding a little.

'My sister, Celia, will love you,' he said at last. 'She is fifteen and I think she is sometimes lonely. She will be glad to have another young woman and a new brother in the house.'

'And your mother?'

The silence was longer this time.

'I'm not sure,' he said abruptly. 'She had plans for me, and may not take it kindly that they cannot be fulfilled now. But I am sure she will like you when she gets to know you.'

It did not sound promising.

'Will they like me?' another voice piped up, and Martin gladly seized the chance to change the conversation.

'Yes, Thomas. You will be able to help me on the home farm. I will teach you to ride properly and then you may have your own pony.'

Thomas sighed blissfully.

At least he will be safe and happy, Lucy thought, and that is why I married Martin. Martin will be home with his family and free to work on his land again, so I think he will be happy. But what about me?

The landscape was changing. High, rolling hills looked down on them as they followed the valley roads, till one day Martin stopped his horse at the top of a pass and looked back at them, his face bright with anticipation.

'Look!' he cried, pointing ahead. 'Radford Hall! We are home.'

3

Lucy looked down at the broad valley. Small cottages dotted the green expanse and a small village, hardly more than a hamlet, was visible where the network of narrow roads was linked. She followed the line indicated by Martin's pointing finger and, near some farm buildings on the outskirts of the village, saw a house larger than any other in the valley.

It was L-shaped. One wing was the black and white architecture of the Tudor dynasty, while a newer, brick wing showed the tall windows and twisted chimneys of the Jacobean style, named after the Scottish James, grandfather of the would-be king now fleeing for his life.

Lucy swallowed. Most of Martin's talk about his home had been about the farms and the tasks waiting for him there, and she had half-expected him to bring her to a farmhouse like those in her own country, a comfortable but unassuming building. Radford Hall, however, was clearly the home of a gentleman. She began to wonder again how the ladies of such a house would receive her.

She had no time to reflect or try to prepare herself. Martin was urging on the horses, eager to reach his home. Soon they had reached Radford Hall. He led them past the front entrance and round to the stables at the end of the Tudor wing.

A girl carrying a basket of apples was crossing the courtyard within the two wings when the horses' hooves began to clatter on the cobbles. She looked up in evident alarm at the unknown intruders. Then Martin waved gladly and she dropped the apples and flew towards him, to be caught in his arms as he dismounted.

'Martin! Martin! We thought you were dead!' the girl sobbed. 'A pedlar brought us news yesterday that King Charles had been defeated at Worcester and thousands of his men killed.'

'But as you can clearly see, sister, I am still alive,' Martin pointed out. 'I'm hungry, thirsty and dusty, but I've come back safe and well. Now, you must meet . . . '

But the girl had whirled away, gathered up her skirts and run for the house. She disappeared inside, calling over her shoulder, 'I'll tell Mother!'

Thomas had slid to the ground and was gazing round with big eyes. Martin helped Lucy to dismount and she was still standing by the horse, smoothing down her skirts, when Celia Radford reappeared, moving with a little more decorum now and accompanied by a tall, dignified figure who swept towards the three as they stood by the horses.

Mistress Radford had a hawk-like face and iron-grey hair under a snow-white cap. She was dressed in black velvet with a gold chain round her neck. Both her wide collar and the cap were of the finest linen with deep borders of fine lace. Although her only son had returned unexpectedly from a battle where so many had died, her face showed no eagerness or pleasure, and in fact she was frowning slightly.

'Martin! Why didn't you send us a message? I would have ordered the servants to make ready and warm your room. And what have you done to your hair?'

She halted. Her eyes had moved from Martin to the two other figures.

'Who are these people?'

Martin moved forward and kissed his mother formally on the cheek. She did not respond, still watching Lucy and Thomas. Martin moved away from his mother and took Lucy by the hand.

'Mother, I bring you a new daughter. This is my wife, Lucy, and her brother, Thomas.'

Mistress Radford stood as if turned to stone. Lucy could imagine how her new daughter-in-law must appear to her. Lucy's grey cape was dusty, her dress was soiled and creased, wisps of hair were escaping from her cap, and she was pale with dark shadows of weariness under her eyes after days of travelling.

'I see,' was all Mistress Radford said.

Martin led Lucy forward and she prepared to embrace the older woman in greeting, but Martin's mother simply turned away as she approached and stalked towards the house. After a moment's hesitation they followed her and found her standing in the hall, hands clasped in front of her in a way that prevented any attempted embraces.

'I gather you have been travelling,' she said without preamble. 'Celia will show you to your rooms so that you may refresh yourselves. We keep country hours here. Dinner will be at four o'clock. I shall see you then.'

She turned and swept away through a door that she shut firmly behind her, leaving the others standing at a loss. Martin was the first to recover, smiling apologetically down at Lucy.

'I'm afraid this has been a shock to Mother. Give her time to recover and I am sure she will greet you properly as my wife.'

Lucy forced herself to smile back, and then turned to Celia Radford who stood by uncertainly.

'Well, at least I can greet my new sister.'

She took Celia's hands and kissed her on both cheeks, and although the girl looked flustered she did not draw away.

'Your mother was right,' Lucy said. 'I am tired and dusty, and we would all like to wash. Where shall we go?'

Celia looked at a loss and Martin took over.

'I can take you to our room. Celia, is the room next to yours fit for Thomas, the one that I used to have when I was a child?'

Given something to do, the girl stirred into action.

'I have kept it in good order. It needs bedding and a fire to warm it, but it is ready otherwise. I'll tell Molly to light a fire and find some sheets.'

She looked at Thomas shyly.

'You are welcome, brother. If you will come with me I am sure I can find something for you to eat as it is still some time to dinner.'

Thomas followed her eagerly, leaving Martin and Lucy alone in the hall until a door opened and a man in serviceable buff jerkin and breeches appeared, smiling broadly.

'Master Martin! Welcome back! I saw you ride past. We have missed you on the farm these past few weeks. I've done what I can but there are many things for you to decide.'

Martin's face reflected the warmth of the greeting.

'John! I'm glad to see you again and I am eager to get back to work.'

The servant's gaze flickered over Lucy and then he turned to his master with a look of enquiry. Martin responded.

'Lucy, this is John Scudamore, who

cares for the estate when I am away. John, this is your new mistress, my wife, Mistress Lucy Radford.'

The look of astonishment on John's face was banished hastily even as Lucy tried to adjust to her new name, and the servant was smiling as warmly at her as he had at Martin.

'You are very welcome, Mistress Radford.'

Lucy felt just a little bit better, and then Martin took her arm.

'We need rest at the moment, John, but I'll be along to see you soon.'

He guided Lucy up the sweeping staircase and along a wide passage, threw open a door and ushered her in.

'This is our room.'

It was a spacious, dignified chamber, with oak panelling and a four-poster bed. The walls were hung with tapestry, and through the big window Lucy could see the green fields stretching away to the hills, but the air was chill, and she shivered.

'I'll get a servant to light a fire and air

the bed with a warming-pan later,'
Martin told her. 'There is a dressing-
room through here and there are closets
and cupboards enough for both our
belongings.'

'All I have is in our saddle-bags,' she
pointed out. 'That will scarcely fill a
shelf.'

He smiled obediently at this, and
then faced her, suddenly solemn.

'You have not been received properly.
My mother is set in her ways, used to
things being ordered as she wants them,
and an unexpected bride must have
been a great shock to her. Please forgive
her and make allowances.'

Lucy lifted an eyebrow.

'If I had been her, suddenly presented with a strange scarecrow of a
daughter-in-law, I think I would have
had hysterics. Of course I can understand how she feels.'

Martin looked relieved and grateful.

'Would you mind if I left you to
unpack and make your toilet? I would
like to have a few words with John.'

Soon after he left, a young maidservant, inspired either by Celia or by curiosity, appeared with kindling and lit a fire, and then reappeared with hot water and towels. Alone for the first time since she had left Worcester, Lucy washed and changed her linen and felt much better. When there was a nervous tap on the door she opened it to find Celia hovering outside.

'Come in,' she said welcomingly.

'Thomas likes his room, and his bed is now ready,' Celia said anxiously.

'Thank you,' Lucy said with real gratitude, aware that she had temporarily forgotten her brother as she faced up to her new problems.

'I was glad to help. It will be fun having somebody nearer my own age living here. Martin is nice but he is always busy about the farms and I have been lonely.'

'You have had your mother to keep you company.'

Celia avoided looking at Lucy.

'Yes,' she responded rather hollowly.

So Martin's mother did not show affection to either of her children!

'Anyway, it is nearly four o'clock, time for dinner. Mother insists on punctuality,' Celia said. 'Thomas is waiting for us.'

Thomas was in fact at the top of the staircase and greeted Celia with a grin as if he had known her for years. Lucy's heart lifted. At least her marriage seemed to have achieved the aim of helping Thomas. Celia led the way to the dining-room, a stately chamber with an ornate, plaster roof and heavy, oak furniture. There was the glitter of crystal and silver on the table and sideboard, but Lucy had the eye of an experienced housewife and saw how the shine on some of the polished furniture was dulled by a thin layer of dust. She even noticed a cobweb in one corner of the ceiling.

Mistress Radford was already seated at the head of a long table which could easily have seated twenty. The three newcomers seated themselves near her where places had been laid, and a few seconds later Martin came in and sat beside his mother. At a curt nod from her he said grace, then his mother rang a small silver bell that stood on the table and a bent, old man, who must have been nearly eighty, brought in the dishes of food, shuffling along with agonising slowness.

Lucy realised that in spite of the silver and crystal, the food was plain and homely. Virtually all of it must have come from the farm. There was vegetable broth and stewed mutton, an apple pie and some custards, and a dish of stewed pears. Even a woman who stood on her dignity as much as Mistress Radford finally had to give in to some curiosity about a new daughter-in-law, though at first she did not deign to address Lucy directly.

'Your courtship must have been brief, Martin. As far as I know, you were not thinking of marriage when you left here.'

Martin smiled.

'Indeed I wasn't. But after I met Lucy in Worcester I could not leave the city without her.'

Clever! The truth, but not the whole truth by any means, Lucy thought.

Mistress Radford looked at Lucy's gown with narrowed eyes.

'I know that you must have dressed simply to travel, but one might think from your dress that you were a Puritan.'

'My family have supported the Puritan beliefs,' Lucy responded. 'However, none of them has taken up arms for them.'

Martin's mother gave her son a scorching glance, but he was eating steadily and failed to notice it.

'This family of yours, what is its standing? Where are your estates?'

'Thomas and I are all that are left of the family. My father was a respectable citizen, a merchant. There are no estates.'

'Your father was in trade! But at least you have money.'

Her tone implied that money would be the only thing that would make a Puritan tradesman's daughter remotely acceptable, but Lucy shook her head.

'Unfortunately my father lost all his money in unwise investments some time ago.'

The rest of the meal was eaten in virtual silence, apart from Martin's few remarks to Lucy and his attempts to make conversation with an overawed Thomas. Martin excused himself before the end of the meal, saying that there were urgent matters to attend to on the farm.

Mistress Radford indicated the end of the meal by rising in stately dignity. Lucy decided to try to appeal to her through praise of her home.

'This is obviously a beautiful house,' she commented. 'Would you be kind enough to show it to me?'

Mistress Radford flicked a cold glance at her.

'I am afraid I have other things to do. Celia can show you around.'

The manservant held the door open for her and shuffled through after her, closing it behind him, leaving the other three to their own devices. Lucy turned to Thomas.

'So our new sister is going to show us our new home. Let us follow her!'

She held out a hand to Celia.

'Come, sister. I know Martin loves this house. Show us why.'

An hour later, Lucy knew a lot more about the house, which was important, and Celia was on very friendly terms with Lucy and Thomas, which was probably even more important. The tour had been very enlightening. The house had obviously been the home of a prosperous family for some time and the rooms were pleasant and well-proportioned, though not particularly grand, particularly in the Tudor wing. The furniture was good and solidly made and had obviously been acquired over many years. But overall there was a sense of neglect, and in the older part there were even some signs of decay.

Rooms had evidently been shut up and left untouched for years, and more than once there was the sound of startled mice scuttling for shelter when the door was opened. Lucy considered that an occasional fire and airing the rooms regularly would have kept the damp at bay at least, and it added to her belief that her new mother-in-law was not a good housewife. Celia indicated the doors to her mother's rooms, and Lucy realised that Mistress Radford must have the chief bedchamber and a very sizeable private parlour.

'There are still the kitchens and storerooms,' Celia pointed out, but Thomas had seen enough and Lucy was growing tired.

'Let us leave them for another day.'

Supper was a relaxed, informal meal served by the young maid, who looked at Lucy and her brother with open curiosity. Apparently Mistress Radford took her supper alone in her parlour.

'What do you think of Radford Hall?' Martin enquired, back from the farm in time to share the meal.

'It's a house to be proud of,' Lucy said diplomatically, and he looked gratified.

'You should have seen it when I was young, before this war caused so many difficulties. But I'll have it in order again one day!'

Celia had her own questions.

'You went away to fight for King Charles, Martin, but you've come home with a Puritan bride. How did that happen?'

Martin and Lucy looked at each other.

'One day he just appeared at my door, and I soon knew we were meant for each other,' Lucy said airily.

'How romantic!' Celia sighed.

Finally Thomas and Celia were ordered off to bed. Martin sat lingering over a glass of wine.

'I gather Celia showed you the house, not my mother.'

'Celia is younger, with more energy.'

'Mother can be difficult. Her father

54

was knighted by King James on his way south to London when he succeeded to the throne, and I sometimes feel that that was the high point of her life. Since my father died three years ago, she has had few people to talk to whom she considers her equal. She has spent too much time alone brooding on her pride and the disappointments she has suffered.'

'And now you have come home with a penniless Puritan bride. Well, it is clear the house needs another pair of hands and I am willing to work hard in return for my board and lodging.'

He looked at her, startled.

'You are not a servant earning your keep. You are my wife.'

She remembered his words as they mounted the staircase towards their bedroom. The room was warm and cosy now, and there was clean water and towels in the dressing-room where Lucy undressed and put on her simple nightgown. Looking in the mirror, she regarded herself gravely.

'This is your true wedding night,' she said to her reflection. 'This is when you truly become Mistress Lucy Radford.'

She lay waiting in the great bed while Martin in his turn washed and disrobed in the dressing-room. She tensed as he came back into the bedroom, blew out the candles, turned back the covers and slipped between them. But he left at least a foot of space between himself and Lucy.

'Good-night. Sleep well,' he said, and turned on his side, his back towards her.

Soon she could tell by his quiet breathing that he was asleep, but Lucy lay for some time gazing up into the darkness.

4

The next morning, Martin swept a delighted Thomas off to help him in the fields, Celia disappeared unobtrusively, and Lucy was left to her own devices. She had spent some time during the night planning how to soften Mistress Radford, and when that lady finally appeared from her bedchamber Lucy was waiting.

She approached her mother-in-law with a smile that showed no remembrances of yesterday's slights, and contrived a small bob that was almost a curtsey. The older woman was compelled to halt and nod in greeting, albeit rather ungraciously.

'I have kept house for my father for the past three years,' Lucy informed her. 'I thought perhaps I could help you in some way in the housekeeping.'

'Housekeeping?'

The stately eyebrows were raised.

'We have servants to do that.'

Mistress Radford swept into her parlour, leaving Lucy grinding her teeth. Servants? Where were they? All she had seen so far was the ancient butler and the young maid who had served supper. Well, she would try to find these servants. She located what must be the servants' hall, knocked firmly, and walked in without waiting for a reply.

She found herself in a large, low-ceilinged chamber which looked as though it could have accommodated a dozen cooks and their helpers. This morning, however, she could see only a middle-aged woman, the young maid, and Celia, seated at one end of an enormous kitchen table, engaged busily in preparing vegetables. They looked up, startled, as Lucy came towards them.

'I am afraid there was no time to meet you yesterday,' she said, smiling at the middle-aged woman who was clearly the cook.

Celia sprang to make them known to each other.

'This is Agnes Lockyer, Lucy, our cook for several years, and this is Maggie, our maid.'

Lucy sat down and picked up a knife.

'Well, at least I can help while we get to know each other. I can peel a carrot, and I have a light hand at pastry if there is any to be made.'

At first there was almost total silence as they worked, but Lucy asked an occasional question, commented on the size and equipment of the kitchen, and finally as they grew more at their ease with her, she began to put together a picture of the household.

'I remember the time when this kitchen was always full,' Agnes Lockyer told her. 'I had two kitchen-maids, and there were plenty of others busy about the house and the farm. Then the war started, and too many of the younger men in the valley decided to give up life in the valley and enlist in the king's army.'

She sighed heavily and then shrugged resignedly.

'There are still mothers waiting to find out what happened to their sons. Some we know were killed, others have returned maimed and no good for work. Then it became difficult to get our produce to market or get a worthwhile price. Martin and the old master worked hard, but then Master Radford was thrown by a young horse and broke his neck and all the responsibility fell on the young master. He's done his best, but money has been short, as well as labour. At least he's made sure we all have enough to eat, plain fare though it may be.'

'So who is left to look after the house?'

'There's me and Maggie here. Another woman comes in to help when she can, though she spends as much time in the fields now as she does in the house.'

'What about the butler who served us dinner?'

There was a ripple of laughter from all three women.

'Master Bateman came here with Mistress Radford. He should have given up work long ago and been left to nod by the fire, but she insists she must have her butler, so he spends most of his time asleep in his room and I wake him up when it's dinner time.'

Now came the delicate part.

'How has Mistress Radford reacted to these changed circumstances?'

Agnes and Maggie looked at each other while Celia concentrated furiously on peeling apples.

'I don't think she has really accepted that things have altered,' Agnes Lockyer said slowly. 'She issues her orders and assumes they will be carried out. We do what we can, but she doesn't seem to notice what is happening.'

'So long as my mother has her butler and her velvet gowns she is satisfied,' Celia burst out resentfully. 'She spends her days in the parlour, embroidering and writing letters, while I work like a servant about the house.'

'Some women have little taste or talent for the details of running a home,' Lucy said hastily. 'Now, I like to see a room shining and spotless. When this food is prepared, you and I will clean and dust in the dining-room, Maggie.'

The maid looked up hastily and a little resentfully. Mistress Radford's lax supervision had enabled her to fall into lazy ways. She glanced at Agnes Lockyer, who gave her a meaningful glance.

'Mistress Lucy is the young master's wife, Maggie.'

The cook was reminding the girl that as the owner's wife by rights, Lucy was now in charge of the house. In a larger establishment Mistress Radford would have retired to a dower house, leaving Lucy to head the table and issue orders to the servants. Well, Lucy was not going to upset Martin by challenging his mother for supremacy, but at least she was going to see the house was kept decently.

Lucy chattered to Maggie and complimented her on her progress as they worked until the girl's initial resentment vanished and Lucy was able to feel confident that she could be a hard and willing worker.

Dinner was served that day on a table freshly polished with beeswax. The cobwebs and dust had vanished and the wooden floor was fresh and clean, though Mistress Radford either did not notice this when she appeared for dinner or did not deign to comment on it.

During the days that followed, Lucy settled into a routine. When Mistress Radford made her way through the house she must have thought that everything was proceeding as before, but once she was occupied with her affairs in her own rooms Lucy busied herself putting the house in order. The women servants might have resented the work if it had not been for the fact that Lucy worked harder than anyone.

Thomas was happy with Martin, and soon made friends among the village boys. In fact he only complained when Lucy insisted that he should spend some time studying to help his neglected education. Celia blossomed in the company of a young woman who showed an interest in her. Her education had also been neglected since her father had died and her mother gave her no guidance. Lucy tried to spend some time each day instructing her in the arts of housewifery but also reading with her and trying to impart some wider knowledge of the world.

Martin was desperately trying to cope with the preparations necessary for winter, many of which had been neglected because of oversight or lack of labour while he was away. He left the house early each day, often not returning for dinner. After days spent working and without any adult conversation, Lucy came to cherish the hours after supper when Thomas and Celia had retired to their rooms and she and Martin could relax and talk.

'The house has changed since you came here, Lucy,' he told her one evening. 'I have noticed how much better it is now, how well ordered and clean. I am afraid my mother paid little attention to it.'

'If your mother prefers to occupy herself in her room and I am free to look after the house, then we are both happy. It gives me something to do so you needn't worry about me.'

'You've no idea how pleasant it is to know there is something I don't have to worry about. There is too much to do on the farms before winter closes in and too few people to do it. We are working together, treating all the farms as one, but it is still a struggle. The villagers know how urgent it is to get everything done if we are to eat this winter and next year, and all who can have been out helping.'

Lucy knew this. She had helped carry

out food and beer to the fields and was slowly coming to know the other inhabitants of the village. Agnes and Maggie seemed to have given a favourable report on her, for the men and women greeted her pleasantly enough, though she sensed they were withholding judgement till they knew her better.

Several times she had lingered to watch Martin in the fields, stripped to his shirt as he toiled with the other men, with nothing to set him apart from them as a gentleman. His hair was growing again, curling round his ears and she had felt her heart stir as she watched him. The sight of him would please any woman, and she was his wife. But no matter how he appreciated her as a housewife, there was still that gap between them in bed each night.

At least, if she could not repay him with the comfort of her body for the shelter he gave to her and Thomas, she could see his beloved house was cared for. But Lucy found that Mistress

Radford could still cause problems.

At dinner one day she turned her stately head towards the butler.

'Tell the cook that we are expecting guests tomorrow and they will want refreshments.'

As Martin and Lucy looked at her in surprise she spoke to Martin.

'Of course I shall expect you to be here to greet them and to introduce your bride.'

Here she acknowledged Lucy's existence with the shadow of a nod.

'But, Mother, who are these guests? I cannot spare a day from the fields at this time!'

'Nonsense, Martin. I have invited Sir Henry Downing and his wife, and Henrietta, of course. They are old friends and will expect to see you.'

As far as she was concerned, this was obviously the end of the matter, though Lucy could see that Martin was fuming. When the meal was finished she interrogated him anxiously. He explained that the guests were from the next valley, a prosperous couple with one child, their daughter, Henrietta.

'Can you see that we entertain them fittingly?' he asked her anxiously.

She nodded, mentally listing their resources. There would be bread, meat and cheese, of course, but she could prepare apple tarts and custards, and there was enough wine and beer to drink. She would not be able to dazzle the guests with some of the exotic dainties she could have prepared in Worcester, but they would have no cause to complain.

However, there was another problem, not so easily solved. She had brought three plain grey gowns from Worcester and was in the process of making herself another from a bolt of grey-blue cloth she had found. Unfortunately it was still unfinished, and she did not want to present a drab appearance to these unknown neighbours. However, Celia was able to help.

'You have one gown clean and pressed,' she pointed out when Lucy revealed her worries. 'You can borrow a cap and collar which I rarely wear. The linen and lace are both of high quality, and I have some ribbons which you can use to make a bow at the neck. You will look well.'

Lucy relaxed a little.

'Can you tell me anything about the Downing family?'

'They are people I have known all my life. Sir Henry is known to drive a hard bargain at market and men respect him. His wife is pleasant and well-meaning.'

'And the daughter?'

Here Lucy sensed Celia grow evasive.

'Henrietta? She takes after her mother, I suppose. Why don't you ask Martin?'

But Martin worked until dark that day and had no time to talk to his wife.

The next morning was spent in a flurry of activity, readying the house and helping Agnes Lockyer with the refreshments. The guests were expected at noon and would leave about three so that they could get home before it grew too dark. Three hours would not be long, Lucy thought. Perhaps she could make friends with Henrietta. It would be pleasant to have someone to visit.

Just before noon, Martin was already in the hall, dressed in his best coat. He looked up as Lucy came down the staircase and his eyebrows rose in appreciation. He stepped forward and took her hand.

'At least our guests will see that I have brought home a pretty bride.'

'We will soon find out what they think,' his mother's cold voice said as she left her parlour to join them. 'Their carriage is nearly here.'

In fact the wheels could be heard on the drive. The front door was thrown open and Martin went to greet their guests while Lucy and Mistress Radford waited in the doorway. A well-built man in late middle age had accompanied the carriage on horse-back, and he was the first to greet Martin, slapping him on the back after he'd given up his horse to John

Scudamore, who had been pressed into service as a groom for the visit. Then Sir Henry Downing helped his lady from the carriage, and Lucy, good Puritan though she was, looked a little enviously at the blue velvet dress and matching fur-edged cape.

Both parents turned back to the carriage and Martin gave his hand to a third figure, obviously Henrietta Downing. As Henrietta stood on the drive, looking expectantly at the house, a shaft of autumnal sunshine lit her. Lucy felt herself grow cold and knew that Mistress Radford was looking at her with sly triumph.

Henrietta Downing was probably eighteen years old, slender, and of medium height. Her hair was corn gold, and her large blue eyes were veiled with long lashes. Lucy had always thought that the idea of a complexion like a wild rose was merely a poetic flight of fancy until she saw Henrietta.

She welcomed the visitors with a smile, however, and they were taken into the parlour where both Sir Henry and Lady Downing fussed over their daughter, anxious that she should be seated comfortably and away from any draughts. Henrietta smiled placidly and accepted their concern as her due. Her rose pink gown trimmed with swansdown matched the colour of her cheeks and full lips. Lucy thought she had never seen a girl as beautiful as Henrietta. No wonder her parents cherished her, and no wonder Martin could not take his eyes off her!

Sir Henry Downing, however, did remember the purpose of their visit. He kissed Lucy on the cheek and told her she was a very pretty bride, shook Thomas by the hand and told him he must come hunting with them the following year, complimented Celia on her growth, and showed Mistress Radford exactly the kind of respectful admiration she liked.

Martin responded well, man to man, and Lucy began to relax. Even though Henrietta was one of the loveliest girls, she would be going home in a few hours and she herself would no longer feel so dowdy in contrast. The refreshments were brought in and conversation became more general. Sir Henry, after asking Martin a little about his experiences in Worcester, turned to Lucy with an easy flow of small talk which needed little response. Then, during a lull in their conversation, she heard Mistress Radford speaking to Lady Downing loudly enough to be heard by everyone.

'A Puritan, her father was in the trade, and she hasn't a penny to her name. Not what you and I had hoped,' she was saying and she looked meaningfully at Henrietta.

Sir Henry looked taken aback. The colour rose in Lucy's cheeks, but she responded to Sir Henry's last comment as if she had not heard her mother-in-law's unfortunate remarks and he gladly followed her lead, continuing to chat easily. Martin's eyes were sparkling with indignation, however, but he followed Lucy's example and ignored his mother's unfortunate remarks.

Punctually at three o'clock the guests took their leave. Mistress Radford vanished into her own apartments as if aware that she had gone too far and might be challenged. She sent a message via Maggie to say that the visit had tired her and she would dine in her room.

When they were alone together that night, Martin, still angry, apologised to Lucy for his mother's behaviour.

'You should have told me how my mother was behaving to you. I thought she was reconciled to you as my wife, but she has grown arrogant in these last few years with no-one to cross her. She is usually careful not to go too far in front of me but her behaviour today was unforgivable and I must speak to her about it.'

Lucy, tired and heartsick, shook her head.

'Why shouldn't she say what she feels, especially when it's true? When

I forced you into marriage I was thinking only of Thomas and myself. I didn't realise that you might wish to marry someone else. You intended to marry Henrietta, didn't you?'

He hesitated, and then answered reluctantly.

'My parents wished me to marry her. It would have been a good match, and I suppose I took it for granted that someday we would marry, but nothing had been said. After all, the girl is still very young.'

'No wonder your mother cannot bear me,' she said bitterly. 'She expected you to marry a girl she knew and approved of, a beautiful young heiress. Instead she's got a low-born, plain, penniless Puritan.'

'Don't talk like that!' Martin's hands nearly crushed hers. 'You are my wife, a good wife and a tower of strength! Look what you have done to the house, and how happy Celia is with you as a sister.'

But he did not say that she was pretty, Lucy noted. She was useful to him, but he did not look at her as he had looked at that fair-haired girl.

'You must hate me,' she said dismally, unable to stop the tears trickling down her cheeks.

'No!' he replied. 'Let me tell you about my mother. She loved my father, even though she thought she had married beneath her. When he died I was almost overwhelmed, forced to take on a double load before I was really ready for it and I had no time to spare to comfort her. My mother was left a lonely woman with no-one to keep a check on her pride. I was sorry for her, and anyway it was easier to let her lead her life as she wished. It wasn't harming anyone. So now she spends her days dreaming of the way of life she thinks should have been hers. She embroiders and writes letters to members of the aristocracy who have never heard of her and rarely reply, ignoring the fact that until you came, the house was decaying around her. Once, however, she did us real harm.'

He poured them both another glass of wine.

'After my father's death we had some money in our strongbox. In addition to what my father had left me I had managed to sell some stock at a good price and it looked as though I would be able to afford a new breeding bull. I planned to buy myself a better horse as well and went to the strongbox to see just how much money there was. It was empty.'

Lucy waited for him to go on.

'I found out what while I'd been away for a couple of days, two strangers had come to the house. Apparently they told my mother that Charles Stuart was in desperate need of money and was appealing to all good Royalists to help him. She still had my father's key to the strongbox. She opened it and gave them everything. They vanished without even giving her anything to acknowledge what they had received. It left us almost penniless and I doubt if any of it ever reached Charles Stuart. So you see, my mother is a lonely, embittered and rather foolish woman, but in spite of that I will not let her make you unhappy.'

Lucy placed a hand on his sleeve.

'If you want me to be happy, don't say anything to her,' she begged. 'She may feel sorry for her behaviour when she has time to think. If you reproach her, she will only resent me more.'

He put a comforting arm round her shoulders.

'Are you sure? If that is really what you want, I will say nothing this time, but if I ever find that she is slighting or insulting you again I shall remind her that I am master of the house now, and you are my wife. Come to bed now, Lucy. You are tired. Tomorrow life will resume its usual pattern of work in the fields and the house and we can forget our visitors.'

Slowly she mounted the stairs. Mistress Radford's behaviour could be forgotten, but Lucy would never be able to forget the way Martin had looked at Henrietta Downing. If only he would look at her like that! But he regarded her simply as a friend and companion.

5

Winter was closing in on the Derby-shire valley. As the winds swept down from the hills Lucy longed for Worcester where the countryside was so much gentler and friendlier. Here the house was made secure against the gales and log fires roared in the hearth to keep the cold at bay.

Lucy was lonely. Even with the animals brought down safely from the hills there always seemed to be something for Martin to do. Thomas was happier than he had ever been, his time divided between schooling and helping Martin, and he had formed a close friendship with Jack, John Scudamore's son. Although Lucy's brother and Celia seemed to have forgotten that they had not been together from birth and Celia worked readily in the house alongside Lucy, she was too young to be a real companion to her.

Mistress Radford seemed to be keeping to her own rooms more and more, appearing only for dinner and apparently content to leave the effective running of the house to Lucy, who felt that she regarded her as a convenient housekeeper rather than a daughter-in-law. Her manner towards Lucy was patronising and barely polite, except when Martin was present. Then she was careful to observe the formal courtesies.

Lucy found an unexpected outlet for her energies after she found the maid, Maggie, white-faced and in pain one day.

'It's my ear! The pain won't let me sleep!'

Lucy remembered how Thomas had been treated once for earache.

'Let us go to the kitchen and ask Agnes to roast an onion for you.'

'What good will that do?' the sufferer asked querulously.

But after she had experienced the

comfort of the hot onion held against her painful ear she must have praised Lucy to the villagers, for Lucy found that they started coming to her for advice on how to treat petty ailments. Much of what she told them to do was just good sense, things that she had heard about or learned from experience, but she found an old book, handwritten by a former mistress of Radford Hall, which interspersed simple remedies among cooking recipes and Lucy consulted this when necessary.

Most of the herbs required grew in the gardens. There was feverfew for a fever or headache, and an infusion of camomile helped those who could not sleep. The villagers discovered, too, that Lucy did not flinch when faced with an ugly wound. She bandaged limbs neatly and deftly, and they grew to respect her more and more. She found out which families had lost their men folk in accidents or the wars, and saw that bread and other staples were provided for them unobtrusively.

The Puritan Parliament had abolished Christmas in 1647, denouncing the riotous festivities and pagan associations. It had been made illegal to exchange gifts, light a candle or sing Christmas carols. In Radford Hall's remote valley, however, the festival was still celebrated defiantly. In spite of Mistress Radford's sneers about the Puritan attitude, Lucy decided to take part in the festivities.

'Thomas has heard all sorts of stories from his friends about the feasting and presents,' she told Martin. 'I am not going to tell him that he and I are going to sit miserably apart while all his friends enjoy themselves.'

So she made puddings and dressed meat for the festival.

'I think I'm going to enjoy celebrating this feast,' she commented to Agnes Lockyer as they chopped and stirred one morning.

The cook paused for a moment.

'Perhaps next year we'll have even

more to celebrate,' she said significantly.

Lucy was puzzled. Was Agnes talking about the Royalist cause? Surely there was no hope for that any more. The cook resumed her labours.

'It's a fine thing to celebrate the birth of the baby Jesus, but the birth of a son to you and Master Martin would have the whole valley rejoicing.'

Lucy went scarlet.

'I can't promise you that!'

The cook shrugged.

'Well, you had a fine romantic start, falling in love and getting married within a week. A child would make everything complete.'

Inwardly Lucy agreed, but her heart ached at the thought that that particular dream seemed very unlikely to come true.

On Christmas Day, Lucy gave Thomas a riding whip which Martin had managed to buy, delighted Celia with a beautifully-embroidered petticoat, gave her husband two new shirts which she had made herself, and even presented Mistress Radford with some fruit which she had candied herself. At dinner on Christmas Day, wearing the new dress she had made herself, she surveyed her family around the table and told herself that she was content, or almost content.

Before the meal Martin had sought her out.

'Don't you think you deserve a present?' he had challenged her.

'Presents are always welcome, though I wouldn't say I deserve one.'

'But I think you have earned one. Keep still.'

He drew a small, leather bag from his pocket and extracted a single strand of pearls.

'My first Christmas present to my wife.'

He fastened the clasp around her neck.

'My father gave them to me many years ago and told me to give them to the woman I married.'

She looked down at the shining, iridescent pearls in wonder.

'Thank you,' she whispered.

He saw the tears in her eyes and gently wiped them away with one finger.

'I hoped to make you happy, not make you weep.'

'People cry with happiness.'

He smiled down at her tenderly.

'A year ago I didn't know you, Lucy, but now I can't imagine how I could cope without you. We met as enemies, but we have become friends, and I hope we will remain so.'

He produced a sprig of greenery and held it over her head.

'What is that?'

'Mistletoe. If you kiss someone under the mistletoe at Christmas, it is a pledge of friendship.'

She closed her eyes and held up her face. He bent and kissed her lips gently.

'Merry Christmas, my dearest friend.'

She would have to be satisfied with

that, although by now she knew she wanted him as a lover, a true husband.

After the brief cheer of Christmas, winter seemed even grimmer. Snow fell, gradually piling higher and higher, until it was impossible to reach some of the stock. One morning John Scudamore sought out Martin. He looked troubled and anxious.

'There are six sheep missing,' he told him. 'I think the wind drove them before it last night, and it looks as if they are somewhere to the north. Shall I take two or three men and try to find them?'

Martin looked up sharply. Six sheep would be a major loss. Then he looked out the window at the leaden sky and shook his head slowly.

'It's too late. There'll be more snow within the hour. There's a chance the sheep will find some hollow to shelter in.'

'But they might freeze to death!' Thomas said, already aware of what a bad winter could do to stock.

'A man's life is more important than that of a sheep,' Martin told him.

Thomas did not appear for dinner that day. This was not a rare occurrence, as quite often he preferred to eat among the cheerful informality of the Scudamore family rather than under the cold gaze of Mistress Radford, although he usually told Lucy first. However, soon after the meal had concluded, John Scudamore himself made his way through the snow that was now falling steadily, in search of his son. A few questions revealed that neither Jack nor Thomas had been seen for some hours.

'Where can they be?' Lucy said anxiously. 'They can't be outside in this weather.'

Then she saw Celia, wide-eyed, her hand to her mouth.

'What's the matter? Do you know where they have gone?'

'I'm not sure, but they may have gone to look for the missing sheep.'

There was a horrified silence.

'Why do you think that?' Martin asked at last.

'They were saying what a pity it was to leave the sheep to die, and that they were sure they could be rescued. I think they may have wanted to prove they could do it by themselves.'

Lucy felt sick. The wind had risen again, driving the snow against the windows. Two young boys out in this storm would have little chance of survival. Martin looked at her white face and then ordered Celia to check whether Thomas's coat and his heavy boots were missing, while John Scudamore ran home to check in his own house. It was soon clear that the outdoor clothing of both boys was gone, as well as a couple of sheepskin cloaks and two stout sticks.

'They are out on the hills,' John Scudamore groaned.

Martin nodded grimly.

'And if we don't find them soon they won't survive many hours. Go to the village and see if anyone is willing to help us search.'

Within half an hour, a dozen men had set out towards the north side of the valley. All Lucy and Celia could do was wait and pray. Even Mistress Radford paced restlessly up and down the hall, peering through the windows at the swirling snowflakes. Her ancient butler, Bateman, vaguely aware that there was some sort of trouble, followed her closely.

As it grew dark, one of the villagers who had set out with the search party appeared, shaking his head hopelessly.

'We couldn't find them. There were no tracks to follow and we couldn't see where we were going ourselves. When it fell dark Master Martin sent us back. It was well-nigh impossible to keep the lanterns lit in this weather but he and John Scudamore have gone on alone. We are keeping a look-out, and we will go out again as soon as it is light.'

He stood, looking worried and helpless, until Lucy thanked him and told him to thank the other villagers for their efforts. Bravely lying, she said she was sure there would be good news soon. When the man had gone, Lucy sank down into a chair, only to look up abruptly as Mistress Radford strode majestically up to her.

'If my son dies looking for your brat of a brother, I shall hold you guilty of his death,' she said bitterly, and swept away to her own rooms.

Lucy sent the servants to bed, promising to wake them when there was any news, and continued to sit waiting in the chair. When Celia sat on the floor and rested her head on the older girl's knees, Lucy put her arms round her comfortingly.

As the cold hours passed, Celia's head grew heavy as she fell asleep, but Lucy gazed ahead, alert and dry-eyed. She knew that every minute that passed meant that the chances of survival for Martin and her brother grew less. What would happen to her then? She would not be able to stay at Radford Hall, shut up with a vengeful Mistress Radford. As soon as the roads were open she would leave and let fate decide where she went and what became of her. If Thomas and Martin were dead she would not care what happened to her.

It was about two o'clock in the morning that she thought she heard noises somewhere outside the house. She sat up, disturbing Celia who opened her eyes and pushed her hair back from her face.

'Listen!' Lucy commanded.

There were noises, growing louder as they approached the house. Then somebody hammered on the back door before realising that it was unlocked and almost falling into the hall. It was the villager who had told them that Martin and John Scudamore had gone on alone, but now he was a man transformed, his face blazing with joy.

'They've found them!' he shouted. 'They are alive!'

The two girls scrambled to their feet as the door was pushed wide open to admit more villagers. Lucy saw the small figure of Thomas cradled in the arms of one of them, and then saw Martin, grey-faced and exhausted, swaying on his feet.

'We found them,' he whispered. 'I found your brother, Lucy.'

She ran towards him and flung her arms around him. His arms went round her as she kissed him full on the lips. For a moment his embrace tightened and she felt his lips respond to hers. Then he collapsed, and she was on her knees beside him, cradling his head on her breast.

The cook and the maid were roused by the noise and together with Lucy had soon taken capable charge of Martin and Thomas. Their wet clothes were stripped off and they were rubbed hard with linen towels to restore a little warmth and then put into beds ready heated with warming-pans. Thomas had been unconscious, but he stirred as he was put between the sheets and his eyes fluttered open for a moment.

'He'll be all right,' Agnes Lockyer

said comfortingly. 'He's chilled to the bone and probably he was scared out if his wits, but there's no frostbite.'

'What happened to John and his son?' Lucy asked urgently.

'Both safe,' she was told, and burst into grateful tears.

Mistress Radford was given the news with her morning coffee and came to the bedchamber where Lucy was keeping watch over Martin. She did not greet her daughter-in-law but gazed down at her son for a full minute before withdrawing without saying a word.

When Martin finally stirred Lucy brought him breakfast in bed. He thanked her and lay back against the pillows after enquiring anxiously about Thomas.

'We'd given up hope of finding them,' he said soberly, 'but John couldn't go back to his wife without their son and I couldn't face you without Thomas. I think the wind must have driven us in the same direction as it did the sheep last night, because we stumbled over the animals in a little sheltered hollow and then we saw the lads, huddled up together among the sheep to keep warm.'

He managed a smile.

'At least they had the sense to do that. But on the way back I began to wonder if we had the energy left to carry them home.'

'Thomas is awake now,' she told him, 'very grateful to you, as I am.'

Martin was out of bed within a couple of hours, but it took Thomas two days to get enough energy to crawl downstairs. At first he and Jack Scudamore tried to treat the event as a great adventure, but when it had been brought home to them that they had put the lives of several other people at risk as well as their own they became subdued and apologetic.

The incident had one good effect. The shared peril and suspense seemed to bring Lucy and Thomas even closer to Martin and Celia so that they were now a closely-knit family. Of course, there was always one exception. Mistress Radford stayed stubbornly aloof.

6

The February thaw that followed weeks of hard frost brought mud and grey skies, but at least the roads were open again and contact with the outside world was possible. One morning, as Lucy scrubbed at the stone floor of the kitchen, Thomas came flying in, his boots leaving fresh patches of mud on the clean slabs.

'Thomas!' Lucy protested, throwing down her brush furiously, but he was not listening.

'There are soldiers coming, Lucy! Jack Scudamore and I saw them riding along the road towards this house. They will be here in a few minutes!'

She stood up abruptly, housekeeping forgotten.

'What soldiers? How many?'

'Six soldiers, and they were wearing lobsterpot helmets, so they must be

Parliament's men. There are two other men with them, dressed in black.'

Soldiers would not come here by chance. Martin had thought that Parliament would not bother to track down a junior officer, but it looked as if he had been mistaken.

'Run and warn Martin!' she urged. 'Don't let the soldiers see you.'

Thomas had been looking excited, but now he looked slightly scared.

'Have they come for him? Do you think they'll harm him?'

'I don't know, but we must give him a chance to hide if he wants to. Go!'

Thomas had scarcely slipped out the back door in search of Martin when there was a thunderous knocking at the front door. Lucy forced herself to wait until the ancient butler had shuffled slowly to the door and opened it. There was the sound of a voice raised in command and then Master Bateman appeared at the kitchen door, looking agitated.

'Some visitors to see the master,' he

said. 'I told them he was out but they insist they must see him.'

'Thank you, Bateman,' Lucy said steadily. 'You may go now. I will see to the matter.'

The butler retired gratefully to his room, while Lucy, forcing herself to behave calmly, went to greet the newcomers. One of the Roundheads had dismounted to knock on the door and two men wrapped in sober black coats with tall black hats stood behind him while the other soldiers waited a little distance away, holding their horses.

'Are you the mistress of this house?' the soldier demanded.

'I am Mistress Lucy Radford,' she returned. 'My husband, Martin Radford, is the owner.'

The men in black advanced to the door and one of them addressed Lucy politely but coldly.

'Good morning, Mistress Radford. Will you please inform your husband, wherever he is, that we have come to speak with him?'

Lucy stood firm, blocking their entrance.

'My husband is somewhere in the fields, I'm not sure where. If you will tell me why you are here I will send someone to try to find him.'

She heard the rustle of skirts behind her.

'Who are these people?' Mistress Radford demanded, and then lifted her eyebrows indignantly at the sight of the visitors. 'Parliament's men!' she almost spat out. 'We want none of you here! We are loyal subjects of King Charles!'

The two men looked at her, undisturbed.

'We know of your family's sympathies, ma'am. That is why we are here.'

There was the sound of firm footsteps in the hall, and the two men in black looked beyond Mistress Radford to where Martin strode confidently into view, with Thomas tagging anxiously along behind. Martin wore an old sheepskin jerkin and mud-stained breeches above heavy boots, but he confronted the unexpected visitors with dignity.

'Martin,' Lucy began, but his mother cut in.

'Martin, tell these fellows to go away!'

'I am afraid Master Radford cannot do that,' one of the visitors said calmly. 'We are here on official business, sent by Parliament. If you obstruct us in the performance of our duties we have the authority to use force.'

There was a brief silence as the Radfords looked at the six armed men in front of the house and realised that they were helpless.

'I understand your business is with me,' Martin said colourlessly. 'You may come into my study to explain why you are here.'

He led the two men in black into the small, barely-furnished room where he conducted the business of the estate when necessary. Mistress Radford was about to enter behind them, but her son turned to her.

'Even though these men follow Parliament, they have had a hard journey, Mother. Would you please see that they are offered some refreshment and food for their horses if they need it?'

He turned to the two men.

'May I offer you some wine?'

The one who had spoken first shook his head.

'We are here on important business, sir, which you may find unpleasant. We do not wish to be accused later of abusing your hospitality.'

Reluctantly, Mistress Radford had made for the kitchen. Lucy was about to follow her, but Martin beckoned her into the study.

'What affects me will affect my wife, I presume. I would like her to be present.'

The door was closed and the Radfords faced Parliament's messengers. Martin indicated the chairs and they sat. Both men drew out papers from the leather satchels they carried and sorted through until they found documents which they considered relevant.

'First of all, Master Radford,' the spokesman of the pair said, 'I must tell you that we are aware that you followed Charles Stuart when he invaded England with a rabble of Scots and that we are also aware that you fought at Worcester against the forces of Parliament. Do you deny it?'

'Certainly not,' Martin said coldly. 'I am proud of having served my king. However, I must say that I am impressed by your detailed knowledge of the king's army.'

He was rewarded with a wintry smile.

'Parliament recently seized the papers of a certain lord of uncertain loyalties. Among other things we found some letters from your mother expressing her pride in your exploits.'

Lucy closed her eyes for a second, feeling a little sick. So Mistress Radford's constant letter writing had put her own son in danger! Martin leaned back, apparently relaxed, but she saw that the fingers of one hand were gripping the arm of the chair tightly.

'What now? Have you come to arrest me and take me to London for trial? I did not think a junior officer warranted such effort!'

The commissioners looked at him with feigned surprise.

'Why should we do that? There would be little point in having the gaols of England bursting with Royalist soldiers. We are looking to the future of England now.'

Martin let his bewilderment show.

'Then why are you here if not to arrest me?'

The man in black smiled again.

'Martin Radford, as well as killing Parliament's soldiers, Charles Stuart and his army did considerable damage to the country as they passed through. They stole cattle, destroyed crops and ruined buildings, impoverishing many worthy men. As an officer of that army you are held responsible for the behaviour of your troops. It has been decided that you should make what restitution you can to help those who suffered.'

He looked at his documents and carefully placed a finger on one line.

'You will pay a fine of one thousand pounds.'

One thousand pounds! This was an incredibly large sum, much more than the estate's income for a year, and Lucy knew that it was impossible for Martin to pay even half that amount. He had turned pale and leaned forward.

'You have miscalculated. This is a poor estate. We live on what we produce and have little money. Even if I agreed that you had the right to levy such a fine, a thousand pounds is far too much.'

'Parliament has the right to demand compensation, and that is what Parliament has decided you should pay.'

And Parliament had the might to enforce its demands. That was why these men came with an armed escort.

'How soon do you want the money?' Martin asked.

'Within six weeks.'

The time limit was irrelevant. Martin paused before his next question.

'What happens if I cannot pay this compensation in time?'

'Then your estate will be confiscated and sold to whoever is the highest bidder.'

Martin sat silent while the Parliamentary officers looked at him confidently.

'So my family will be evicted and made beggars because of what I did?'

The spokesman did not trouble to answer. Lucy felt furious with them and miserably unhappy for Martin at the same time. What about the consequences for herself and Thomas? Wasn't there anything she could do? Suddenly she found herself on her feet facing the commissioners, cheeks scarlet and eyes sparkling with rage.

'This is nonsense! Everybody knows

that Parliament's army did just as much damage to the country, but you are not fining the Roundhead officers! Admit this is a vengeful punishment for opposing you!'

'Madam,' one commissioner began indignantly, but Lucy ignored him.

'And it's not fair! My brother and I will suffer as well. We will lose our home also, and yet our father was a staunch supporter of Parliament and contributed freely to its funds!'

The two men in black looked at each other, then turned to Lucy.

'Can you prove that? What was your father's name?'

'My father was Henry Wetherby, a respected merchant of Worcester. He died suddenly in London last year, but any trader from Worcester would confirm what I say.'

The commissioner who had said little so far shook his head vigorously, his stern face transformed by a smile.

'There is no need of that! Master Wetherby and I met many times in

London over the years and he was a man I liked and respected. I was most distressed by his sudden death. I presume you are Lucy, the daughter he spoke of, and your brother is Thomas Wetherby.'

He glanced at Martin.

'He never spoke of your betrothal.'

'My husband and I met when Worcester was besieged,' Lucy told him.

The other commissioner was whispering urgently to his companion, who listened and then nodded a little reluctantly.

'Yes, yes, I agree.'

He looked at Lucy and Martin, his face once again cold and composed.

'I am afraid this makes no difference to the compensation you must pay. However, in view of Master Wetherby's support for the cause of Parliament we are prepared to extend the time limit for you to pay to six months.'

A few months' grace, but they would still not be able to find a thousand pounds, and Martin's grim face showed this. The commissioner was frowning at Lucy with obvious bewilderment.

'But I don't understand. If you are Henry Wetherby's daughter you should have no difficulty in paying this money.'

Lucy smiled wryly.

'Perhaps you were not aware that when my father died in London he was there to oversee some business ventures which failed. He left us nothing but debts.'

The crease grew deeper in the commissioner's brow.

'Indeed? I had heard nothing of that. Who told you the venture had failed?'

'He took Walter Johnson, his clerk, with him to London. Walter sent us news of his death and the failure of his enterprises.'

The commissioner jotted something down on one of the papers he carried, then stood up, followed by his companion.

'You have my sympathy for your misfortunes, Mistress Radford, but we are here to inform your husband of Parliament's decision and do not have the authority to change that. If you cannot pay the thousand pounds within six months, Master Radford, your estate will be sequestrated. Will you please tell our escort that we are ready to leave?'

Ten minutes later, Lucy and Martin watched the small group of horsemen ride away back along the muddy track. Mistress Radford found them and demanded to know what had occurred.

'They are fining me for supporting the King. Either I pay them a thousand pounds within six months or I will lose the estate.'

Mistress Radford was silenced momentarily by the calamitous news, and then suddenly she rounded on Lucy.

'These are the people you support! Have you informed any of your Puritan friends that there will be a good estate to be bought cheaply when my son and I are thrown out of our home?'

Martin broke in sharply.

'Mother! That is foolish! You know that if we lose the estate Lucy and Thomas will be homeless as well.'

'Then what will happen? Do you think she'll stay with you when you can no longer even provide a home for her? She'll be back to her own kind then, looking for another fool to look after her and her brother!'

Months of careful behaviour and self-control were forgotten as Lucy flared up at her mother-in-law.

'Don't you realise that this has come about because you betrayed your son? It was what you said in your letters which gave them the grounds to impose the fine! And if you hadn't handed over that money to two tricksters, Martin might have been able to find enough money to pay the fine.'

The two women glared at each other, oblivious of the curious servants who had been attracted to the hall by the sound of raised voices. Martin glanced round desperately and then took charge of the situation.

'Mother, you are upset by the news. I suggest you go to your room and I will send Maggie to you with a hot posset. Lucy, haven't you some tasks to see to?'

Given this way of escape from the situation, both women retreated with what dignity they could muster. An hour later Martin found Lucy furiously polishing furniture in the dining-room and paused to watch her.

'You'll wear it out if you rub so hard,' he observed.

She looked at him defiantly.

'It's one way of getting rid of my anger.'

He sighed heavily.

'Come and sit down, Lucy.'

She sat on one of the chairs while he leaned against the table near her, frowning down at the floor.

'It was unfortunate that you couldn't find some way of getting rid of your anger before you spoke to my mother. I can understand how you felt, but you must know that she will never admit she has done anything wrong. It will just make the situation between the two of you even worse.'

Lucy felt wretched.

'I am truly sorry, but I was desperately upset and angry.'

'I know. I felt the same.'

She looked at him wistfully.

'Is there any hope of raising the money? What if we sell most of our animals?'

But he was shaking his head.

'Not even if we sold every sheep and lamb in the fields would we raise the money.'

'Could you borrow the money? Perhaps Sir Henry Downing would lend it to you?'

The headshake was sharp and decisive this time.

'No. Sir Henry has a good estate, but he would not have anywhere near that much money in coin to spare, and anyway I could never pay him back. If things had been different . . . '

He did not finish the sentence, but Lucy could do it for him. If things had been different, if Martin had been Henrietta Downing's promised husband, then perhaps her father would have made the effort necessary to save his future son-in-law's estate without being too much concerned about repayment. Now there was no such motive.

'What shall we do then?' she asked, and Martin forced a smile.

'We'll do what we can. We'll scrape together every spare penny and hope that Parliament will accept payment on account. Failing that, we'll pray for a miracle.'

7

With the worst of the winter past and a few early lambs bleating in the fields, the people of the valley should have been looking forward to spring. Instead there was a spirit of despondency and hopelessness. By some means, and Lucy suspected it had been Maggie listening at the door, news of the great fine imposed on Martin was generally known, and everyone knew that he could not pay.

What was the point of preparing the ground and caring for the beasts when by the time autumn came the harvest might belong to some stranger who had an eye for a bargain? Some villagers feared that they might be driven off the farms where they had lived all their lives and be replaced by workers more sympathetic to Parliament.

Martin tried his best to raise spirits.

He laughed at their doleful faces and said that talk of eviction was just an empty threat.

'The commissioners will settle for what I can afford to give them. They know full well that no Puritan will want an isolated, rain-soaked valley like this when there are good estates available in the soft south. I shall be here for many years to come.'

But his mood was much grimmer when he talked alone to Lucy.

'The commissioners have named a sum and the time when I must pay it. They may feel that if I fail to pay and they do nothing then it will set a bad example to others who will try to avoid paying their fines. The best I can hope for is more time to pay, and that may mean years of poverty for us.' He sighed. 'I am sorry to have brought you to such a pass, Lucy.'

'Nonsense,' she said vigorously. 'You sound as pessimistic as John Scudamore. We shall manage somehow. What you have done for me and

Thomas is given us a home and a place in a family, and I shall always be grateful for that.'

He managed a smile.

'As I remember, I was in your debt for saving my life, and my mother has scarcely welcomed you with open arms.'

In fact Mistress Radford now did her best to pretend that Lucy did not exist. She kept to her rooms more and more, attended by old Bateman.

'But I am glad you are here, Lucy,' Martin went on, 'for whatever reason. With you I can relax. I don't have to pretend. I can talk to you openly. You are my friend, a true helpmate, a comforter.'

The compliment made her cheeks glow with pride, but as the weeks passed she wished desperately that she could do something more concrete than just offer comfort. She did her best to save every penny she could, economising on everything except food and heating, but the money in the strongbox seemed to mount with painful slowness.

Then, one showery morning towards the end of April, Thomas and his friend, Jack, clattered into Radford Hall to warn Lucy that another visitor was coming, but this time instead of a party of soldiers it was a solitary traveller on a sleek, well-bred horse. Lucy could feel her heart beating hard as she waited for the horseman to reach Radford Hall. Was this a messenger from the commissioners? What else could they possibly demand from Martin?

As the rider drew near the house and saw Lucy waiting at the door he doffed his wide-brimmed black hat in greeting, however, and she saw the flash of white teeth as he smiled at her. She relaxed. He did not look like some petty official eager to bring bad news to a Royalist family. As he swung easily down from his horse and strode towards her she saw that he was tall and well built, with cropped dark hair, and when he reached her he stopped and waited, as if expecting her to say something.

She looked at him carefully, aware that there was something familiar about this man. Then suddenly she gave a little scream and rushed forward, all dignity forgotten as she threw her arms round him in greeting.

'Walter! Walter Thomson!'

'At your service, Mistress Lucy.'

As she stepped back, a little embarrassed by the fervour with which she had greeted her father's former clerk, he bent to kiss her hands.

'What are you doing here? How did you know I was here?' she asked.

Thomas appeared by her side, together with Jack.

'Master Thomson! Can we take your horse round to the stables?' Thomas exclaimed.

Walter Thomson gave his consent and the two lads proudly took charge of his steed while Lucy took him by the arm and led him eagerly indoors, just in time to hear a door close hurriedly and she guessed that Maggie and probably Agnes as well had witnessed her affectionate greeting. Thomas reappeared and announced that the horse had been safely handed over to John Scudamore before Lucy sent him to ask Agnes to send refreshments to her sitting-room.

There, she was able to survey Walter Thomson and notice how he had changed in the past year. She remembered him as polite, quiet and self-effacing, neatly dressed in sombre clothes. She recalled describing him once as her father's shadow.

Now, however, he seemed to have grown, or maybe it just seemed like that because he walked so confidently with his head held high. Although his clothes were subdued, they were of excellent woollen cloth and his boots were well made in fine leather. He had evidently prospered.

'I learned you were here by sheer chance,' he said in answer to her questions. 'First, I must tell you that it was always my intention to return to Worcester, to tell you all I could about what had happened to your father, but I could not get back there until after Charles Stuart's rebels had been defeated. Then, when I did get there, I found strangers in your house and all that the neighbours could tell me was that you and Thomas had left with some strange manservant to visit your aunt in Evesham. I knew you had no relatives there and nobody in Evesham remembered seeing you. I went back to London thinking I would never see you again. Then by sheer chance I recently encountered a man who is one of Parliament's commissioners, and he mentioned that Master Wetherby's daughter was now married and living in Derbyshire. Well, as I have business to see to in Matlock I decided to take the opportunity to come and visit you before I went there.'

'I'm so pleased you did! It's wonderful to see a friend from Worcester! It seems you have prospered, Master Thomson.'

He received her compliment a little

smugly, but then a shadow crossed his face.

'If only your father could have done as well! He seemed to have lost his business judgement, unfortunately, and was too eager to risk everything on dangerous projects, as though he were desperate to recoup his losses. Perhaps he was already ill and that affected him. It was one morning after he had received particularly bad news that I went to his room when he did not come down at his usual time and found him dead in his bed. I am sure he died in his sleep, without any pain.'

Lucy bowed her head, tears in her eyes, and then forced herself to look up and smile.

'Thank you for arranging his burial, Walter. What happened to you afterwards?'

'At first I was desolate. I had lost my employment together with my master and friend, but then I found that there was plenty of work in London for a competent man. When I had accumulated a little money I speculated on my own account and I was more fortunate that your father.'

'You look prosperous.'

'I always wanted to own good clothes. Now tell me how you came to marry and move here.'

She gave a suitably edited version of her story, emphasising how happy and content she was, but even while she spoke she could see him looking around and noting the faded hangings and worn upholstery, as well as her own well-worn and darned clothes. Martin was out on the hills and would not be back till late, so she entertained Walter Thomson to a mid-day meal during which she, Celia and Thomas plied him with questions about the great city of London.

After the meal, he announced that he had matters to discuss with Lucy. When they were alone Walter Thomson produced a sheaf of papers.

'These were your father's, so I must

pass them to your care, though I am afraid they are of little importance or value.'

There were a few letters to do with business and some memoranda of his affairs. Lucy's eyes prickled with tears when she found her own letters, full of the details of their quiet life in Worcester. There was one document decorated with a red wax seal, and it proved to be her father's Will, in which he bequeathed two-thirds of his fortune to Thomas and one-third to Lucy, as well as a few minor legacies to friends.

'He meant to leave me a generous dowry,' Lucy commented. 'He was not to know that he would die in debt.'

'But fortunately you have married landed gentry, so I take it you have no more money worries.'

She looked at him reproachfully.

'You know better than that. I saw you looking at the state of the rooms. In fact, we are in desperate need of money.'

She poured out the tale of the

Parliamentary commissioners and the demand for a thousand pounds.

'So you see, we are in deep trouble,' she finished and looked at him wistfully. 'If you have indeed prospered, I wonder if you could make a loan to us. We would pay it back, with interest of course.'

Walter Thomson was shaking his head regretfully.

'What money I have is invested. I will have none to spare for some time.'

'I should not have asked you,' she said, angry with herself for giving way to the impulse.

'If I had the money it would be yours for the sake of your father. He was a good man,' Walter Thomson said quietly, taking her hands.

So it was that Martin entered without warning and found his wife hand-in-hand with a handsome young man, smiling tenderly up at the stranger. As soon as she saw him, Lucy abruptly took her hands from Walter's and stepped back. Martin, stony-faced, waited for her to speak, but she felt flustered by his sudden appearance.

'Martin, this is Walter Thomson who was with my father when he died. Walter, this is my husband, Martin Radford.'

Walter Thomson bowed with a fine flourish, but Martin simply nodded.

'I am Martin Radford, of Radford Hall. So you are the servant who found your master dead.'

Lucy gasped. The greeting was ungracious, impolite, and she would never have believed that Martin could behave so. Walter Thomson's eyes narrowed.

'I was his servant. I am now a merchant in my own right.'

'Master Thomson has business in Matlock,' Lucy interjected.

'Indeed?' Martin said with icy formality. 'Then I take it he will be leaving immediately if he wishes to reach the town before nightfall.'

Lucy had been sure that Martin would offer Walter Thomson a bed for the night and had looked forward to reminiscing about her father. Walter was the only remaining link with the happy days in Worcester.

'I had been preparing to leave,' Walter said smoothly, and he turned and smiled down at Lucy, temporarily ignoring Martin. 'Now I have given you your father's papers there is little left for me to do. There is just one small matter, however. When your father died I had to spend the little money he had left on his funeral expenses and the rest due for his accommodation. I had to do this without authority, and I should be grateful if you would sign a statement I have drawn up stating that you accept my right to take the money. It is a small thing, but it would tidy up a loose end.'

'I'll do so willingly. I only wish there had been enough to reward you for your loyal service,' Lucy said warmly, trying to compensate for Martin's behaviour.

Her husband stood glowering as

Walter Thomson spread out a small document on the table and produced a small travelling inkwell into which he dipped a quill pen before offering it to Lucy. Then, suddenly, Martin strode forward.

'As Mistress Radford's husband I should inspect any documents before she signs them.'

'Really, Martin!' Lucy said indignantly, but Walter Thomson only smiled as he turned to face Martin, his hand grasping and crumpling the document he had offered for Lucy's signature.

'It is not important. I was being over-punctilious.'

Before anyone knew what he was going to do, Walter Thomson had tossed the paper into the fire burning on the hearth then turned to Lucy.

'Thank you for your welcome, Mistress Radford,' he said. 'You have my wishes for your future happiness.'

Then he strode past Martin, calling for Thomas, whom he cheerfully instructed to bring out his horse.

Husband and wife were left confronting each other.

'Your behaviour was unforgivable,' Lucy snapped, high flashes of anger flaming in her cheeks.

'Really?' Martin returned as sharply. 'Am I supposed to welcome a servant as if he were an equal? Anyway, I gather my wife's welcome was warm enough to compensate for mine!'

Lucy remembered the way she had impulsively embraced Walter Thomson and blushed even more, but she held her chin defiantly high as Martin bent over the hearth and picked up the half-burned scrap of paper and smoothed it out, frowning as he tried to decipher it.

'For a careful and punctilious man he has been strangely careless. There is no record here of how much of your father's money he spent.'

'I don't care if he kept a few sovereigns for himself when he needed them. He reminded me of the days when I was happy! John Scudamore is your servant, but I know you regard him as your friend. Now, with your leave, I have matters to attend to!'

She swept past Martin into her sitting-room. From the window, she saw Walter Thomson ride off, accompanied for part of the way by Thomas and Jack Scudamore. He did not look back, and angrily she hammered her fists on the windowsill. She would never forgive Martin!

Had she stayed to think, or if she had had more experience of men, she might have realised that Martin's behaviour showed all the symptoms of a deeply jealous man. Instead she saw it as an echo of his mother's contempt for those who engaged in trade.

Dinner was a miserable meal. Thomas had gone off with Jack, Celia was sulking because the handsome stranger had gone without saying goodbye to her, and Martin and Lucy ate silently with her eyes fixed on their plates. Only Mistress Radford seemed in a good humour, and Lucy suspected correctly that this was because Maggie had reported to her that Martin and Lucy had quarrelled. Later Martin sought out Lucy as she sat mending some of Thomas's clothes.

'I want to apologise for my behaviour,' he began abruptly. 'I know it was unjustified and unworthy of me.'

He paused, but Lucy did not look up or respond in any way. He ploughed on doggedly.

'You know how this fine is preying on my mind and I am weary of pretending to everyone that all will end happily. Then I heard that there was yet another Puritan at my house and I was afraid that Parliament had decided to demand the money now, so I trudged back in my old trousers and jacket, my boots leaking and my heart aching, and found some smooth, well-fed fellow who had obviously never had to work hard, with his hands embracing you and smiling down at you, and you looked so happy to be with him. I was angry and ill mannered, Lucy. Please forgive me.'

Her lips were quivering and her eyes were filling with tears. She knew that if she looked up at him she would break down completely, so pride kept her eyes stubbornly on the sewing in her lap until at last she heard Martin sigh heavily and the door close behind him.

Then she threw the sewing across the room and burst into tears.

8

Celia had shot up over the past few months, and her skirts no longer covered her ankles. Now turned sixteen, she was sufficiently aware of her femininity to desire clothes which fitted and became her.

'I can't wear this dress any more. It looks ridiculous!'

'We could add a false hem, or lengthen it with fabric from an old dress.'

'I would look like a beggar dressed in patches! Surely I can have one new dress!'

Lucy, kneeling beside her to examine the offending garment, wished earnestly that she could buy her young sister-in-law something new and pretty. It would be such a relief to see someone happy.

Ever since Walter Thomson's visit two weeks ago she and Martin had been treating each other with cold politeness. There were no more cosy chats after supper and in fact they did not speak to each other more than was necessary. It was a busy time in the valley, anyway, and Martin worked from dawn to dusk, as if physical exertion and exhaustion might stop him thinking of his problems.

Celia slid down to the floor beside Lucy and enveloped her in a hug.

'I'm sorry! What's an old dress when we have so much else demanding money? Cheer up! You look so pale and tired nowadays. Martin will think of something.'

Lucy kissed her, wishing she could share in her youthful optimism. Time was passing so fast and no miracle had yet happened to produce a thousand pounds.

'What shall we do if the worst does happen?' Celia asked tentatively, revealing her secret worries. 'Where shall we go if we lose Radford Hall?'

'We'll have the whole wide world to

choose from,' Lucy said firmly. 'We could go to France, to the court of King Louis. He is sheltering many Royalists. A French nobleman might fall in love with you and we could all go and live in his chateau. I hear it's warm and sunny in France, which will make a change from this rainy valley.'

They were laughing together when they heard voices from the entrance hall, and within seconds Maggie was knocking on the door, agog with news.

'Sir Henry Downing is here, Mistress Radford. He and the master met on the road. They are in the drawing-room.'

'We'll come at once,' Lucy said, leaping to her feet.

Sir Henry had not visited them since that first time she had met him, and she wondered what had occasioned this call. Entering the drawing-room she was immediately aware that at least it was not to bring bad news. Both men were smiling and Martin was pouring wine and holding up his glass as if for a toast. Mistress Radford, drawn from her rooms by curiosity, was already there and addressing Sir Henry in measured tones.

'You have my congratulations, Sir Henry. It will be a fine match.'

Sir Henry greeted Lucy and Celia with a deep bow.

'Two more beautiful ladies to share my good news! My daughter, Henrietta, is betrothed to William Crossleigh, the eldest son of Sir Joseph Crossleigh, and I am come to bid you to a celebration in two weeks' time.'

So the lovely Henrietta had found a suitable mate! Lucy congratulated Sir Henry and asked him to convey her best wishes to the happy couple, but her thoughts were with Martin. How would he react to the news that the girl he had wanted to marry was now pledged to someone else?

Sir Henry was giving more details of the celebration. He described it airily as a small affair, but as Lucy listened to the roll call of guests she realised that it was intended to be an impressive event, one which would display the fortune and good prospects of the Downings to the rest of the county. But how could the Radfords go? Mistress Radford had some fine gowns and Martin had a good suit of clothes carefully stored away, but how could she and Celia go in their old dresses? And Thomas needed new clothes as well.

There was nothing she could do but listen as Martin accepted the invitation before Sir Henry left to spread his good news farther afield. Mistress Radford was obviously pleased at the prospect of meeting so many of the gentry again on what promised to be a splendid occasion. Instead of rising from the table as soon as supper was finished that night, Lucy turned to her husband.

'Martin, I must speak to you about this invitation from Sir Henry Downing. You and your mother can represent the Radfords, but Celia and Thomas cannot go, and neither can I. We have nothing suitable to wear.'

Martin smiled at her.

'Then get something.'

She frowned in bewilderment.

'You don't understand. Clothes for such an occasion are expensive.'

Martin stretched out his long legs and looked at her ruefully.

'Lucy, what is the point of scrimping and saving when I can't raise even half the money that Parliament has demanded? You and Celia deserve a treat after this winter. Thomas can't run around in rags. Get new gowns.'

She began to protest, and then stopped. It would be pleasant to get away from the endless round of housekeeping and economising and go to the gathering at the Downings' in a new gown. A smile curved her lips.

'Celia is growing into a very pretty girl,' she said. 'It would do her good to find herself admired.'

'Celia is not the only pretty Radford. I look forward to displaying my wife to the county gentlefolk.'

She rose and swept a deep curtsey.

'Thank you for your compliment, sir.'

'I should pay you more. Your eyes sparkle when you are pleased. Now tell me what you want and I will ride to Matlock tomorrow.'

One step at least had been taken on the path to reconciliation.

Both Celia and Lucy were waiting eagerly when he returned from Matlock. He had brought the good dark woollen cloth needed for Thomas's suit, but they gasped with delight when he opened his other parcels. He had brought pale blue silk for Celia, as Lucy had requested, but when he opened the last parcel a torrent of green silk poured out.

'I know you told me to buy pearl grey, but I think this will suit you better,' Martin told her.

Lucy put out a hand and stroked the rich fabric, the vivid green of the fresh leaves beginning to show on the trees.

'It's so beautiful,' she breathed.

She set to work together with Celia and Maggie, and it was soon decided Lucy and Celia had gowns of similar design, with skirts of deep folds flowing from tight basques, but Celia's pale blue fabric emphasised the blue of her eyes. When completed, Lucy handled the brilliant fabric of her own gown lovingly and told herself that abandoning more subdued colours, especially when the design was so modest, did not compromise her Puritan principals.

When the big day came, Lucy looked round at the family gathered together with pride. Mistress Radford was a dignified and impressive figure in black velvet and Thomas looked well in his new suit.

She looked at her husband with special pleasure. He spent so much time in clothes suitable for wearing on the farm that to see him well dressed and looking like a well-bred gentleman was a great treat. Lucy realised that in fact this was the first time that she had seen him dressed as befitted his station since that first day when he had come into her life. He noted her approving look and smiled, offering her his arm.

'We make a good-looking family, don't we? Let us go and impress the Downings.'

John Scudamore had the task of driving Mistress Radford, Celia and Thomas in a pony-cart. Lucy rode pillion behind Martin on one of the horses they had taken from the thieves. It was a beautiful spring day and to be out in the open air riding through the fresh green of the landscape was an enjoyable change. Lucy was aware of Martin's nearness as they jogged along slowly. During the past fortnight they had gradually, a little warily, got back on friendly terms.

'How do you feel?' Martin asked over his shoulder.

'A little nervous,' she confessed. 'I shall be meeting so many strangers.'

'There is nothing to fear. They are my friends and acquaintances, remember, and they will greet you as my wife.'

Lucy nodded, but she knew that though his friends would have welcomed heartily the kind of wife they would have expected Martin to marry, one of their own kind, they would be curious to see the unknown Puritan bride he had brought home so unexpectedly but might not be so kindly disposed towards her.

The journey took two hours, taking them out of the valley of the Radfords, through a break in the hills that normally ringed their horizon, and down into a spacious fertile area. Whereas Radford Hall was definitely the home of a gentleman farmer, Sir Henry Downing's house was a modern building, designed to impress and convey the information that its owner was wealthy enough to employ others to carry out any manual labour and that he would certainly never be found working in the fields himself. Well-manicured lawns and neat gardens surrounded it, as well as a small park.

Today, however, there was no time to admire the building or grounds. A constant stream of guests was arriving and John Scudamore took charge of the pony cart and the horse as the Radfords made their way into the house. The Downings were holding court in the drawing-room, Sir Henry and his wife greeting the guests as they arrived while Henrietta, dressed in white silk, smiled constantly as she stood by her future bridegroom, a floridly handsome young man with shoulder-length fair hair. His parents stood nearby, looking happily self-satisfied.

Sir Henry greeted the Radfords with enthusiasm, asked them if they had ever seen a girl looking lovelier than Henrietta, and pointed out the diamond bracelet she was wearing that was a gift from the Crossleighs.

'Incidentally, Martin,' he said, lowering his voice, 'I have heard about your problems with the Parliamentary commissioners and I would like to speak to you later about that matter.'

Lucy's heart thumped. Surely Martin could not refuse if Sir Henry offered to lend him the money he needed.

Mistress Radford soon spied some

old acquaintances she regarded as being of a satisfactory social status and settled down with them for a good gossip. Celia also knew some of the younger guests and took Thomas to meet them, leaving Martin and Lucy together. She saw a group of ladies looking at her and commenting to each other and grew tense, but then a short, plump lady rose and came to meet them, smiling.

'So, we have a chance to meet your wife at last, Martin Radford. Please introduce us.'

Martin did, and named half-a-dozen other ladies as they flocked round.

'Come and tell us about yourself,' the plump lady said, who had been introduced as Mistress Gosswood. 'Martin, my husband wanted to hear how you had got on at lambing time.'

Thus dismissed, Martin left Lucy to the mercy of the ladies, who proved much friendlier than she had expected. It did not take her long to realise that the rich families of the Downings and the Crossleighs were exceptions, and that most of the local families were minor gentlefolk and farmers like Martin, and that gossip had already given them some knowledge of her. They complimented her on Celia's looks and said what a healthy, well-grown lad Thomas appeared to be.

When Mistress Radford's stately figure was seen in the distance there was a distinct implication that Lucy had their sympathy when it came to dealing with her formidable mother-in-law. She also detected a certain coolness towards the Downings and the Crossleighs.

'Of course, Sir Henry can afford to entertain like this,' one lady said tartly. 'He's driven enough hard bargains in his time to make a tidy profit.'

'Don't worry. I think Mistress Henrietta and young Crossleigh will spend their parents' money fast enough when they get their hands on it,' another said, and some of the others were nodding agreement.

When Martin finally came to claim Lucy she was feeling quite at her ease, promising to visit Mistress Gosswood and others when the summer weather made travelling easier.

Once all the visitors had arrived, musicians began to play and some younger guests began to dance. Lucy could not bring herself to take part in this, but strolled happily through the gardens on Martin's arm until food was served. There were great roast joints of beef, meat pies, fowl of many types, but there was also a fine display of jellies and creams, fruit tarts, junkets, syllabubs and trifles. The table was dominated by a model of a galleon made of almond paste and coloured sugar. Wines and ale accompanied the feast.

By the time the meal was finished, the sun was getting low. Guests were beginning to drift away, eager to get home before nightfall. Lucy, warning Celia and Thomas to be ready to leave soon, saw Sir Henry Downing take Martin by the arm and lead him away from the throng. Watching anxiously, she saw Martin reappear on his own some fifteen minutes later, but it was impossible to tell from his face whether the talk had gone well or not.

Once back at Radford Hall, Mistress Radford went to her own apartments, summoning Maggie to attend on her, and Lucy saw the two youngsters to their rooms where she carefully unlaced and removed Celia's dress and made sure that Thomas's good suit was put away carefully.

Going downstairs, she found Martin sitting in the dining-room, a glass of brandy in front of him. She checked at the sight, for he rarely touched strong spirits. Was he drowning his sorrows after seeing Henrietta with young Crossleigh? He stood up as he saw her and offered her a glass of wine, which she accepted. She had to find out what had happened.

'I saw Sir Henry take you aside,' she began, but Martin did not respond and she leaned forward a little angrily. 'If he offered to help you, that concerns all of us, Martin.'

Martin looked directly at Lucy and she could see the tension in his face.

'Sir Henry Downing told me that he had heard that I had to pay a fine of one thousand pounds or lose Radford Hall and all my lands. He commiserated with me and said he was sure that I would hate to see strangers at Radford, and so would he. He then offered to buy the estate from me for virtually half what it is worth.'

'But I thought he was your friend! Instead he is trying to profit from your misfortune!' Lucy exclaimed.

Martin nodded abruptly.

'Sir Henry has always been known for his good business sense,' he said derisively. 'He was kind enough to say that he would not want to throw me out of the place where my family had lived for so long, and he would be willing to let me stay at Radford Hall, as a tenant farmer!'

Lucy's eyes were sparkling with fury. 'That is not kindness! You know the place better than anyone and you would run it better than anyone. What did you say to him?'

'I thanked him, but said I hoped to solve my problems without resorting to such a drastic solution. He told me his offer would remain open.'

He looked at Lucy unhappily.

'He knows my only hope is to be given more time to pay. I have been thinking that perhaps I should accept his offer. At least it would keep a roof over our heads and my mother would not be forced to leave her home in her old age.'

'Nonsense! How could your mother bear the humiliation of living here as the tenant of a man she regards as no more than her equal! If Parliament won't give you more time to pay then we will leave here together. We are young enough to find work and start again. We could look after your mother and Celia and Thomas would probably think of it as a great adventure. We will face the future together!'

He was smiling now.

'I know what you are capable of, Lucy. I have seen you face my sword, rescue me from certain death and deal with armed robbers. Other people have seen their lives ruined and then rebuilt them. Together we will survive!'

He rose to his feet and she did so, too, instinctively. Then his arms were round her and she was lifting her face to his. It was at this moment that there was a knock on the dining-room door and the old butler, Bateman, shuffled into the room. As Martin and Lucy broke apart he half-bowed.

'Forgive me, Master Radford. I was asleep when you came home. A messenger called today and said this was to be given to you urgently.'

He held out a document fastened with an impressive red seal.

'Thank you, Bateman,' Martin said, waiting till the old man had gone.

Then he looked at the seal and his lips tightened. Carefully he took a knife and broke the seal, then spread the document on the table. When he had read it he closed his eyes and spoke to her dully.

'It is from the Parliamentary commissioners. They order me to report to them in London as soon as possible.'

9

It was almost dawn before Lucy tumbled into bed for a couple of hours of broken sleep. There had been so much to discuss and to plan. The commissioners' summons must be answered as soon as possible. Martin intended to leave the very next day but he would be away several weeks at least and while John Scudamore was a capable second-in-command he was reluctant to take decisions on his own and Martin would have to leave clear instructions for everything he wanted done.

Lucy had gone through Martin's scanty wardrobe to see what he should pack, grateful that she had never left any mending or darning for another time. Martin would leave with three hundred golden sovereigns. He would offer that to the commissioners as a preliminary payment, and what happened next would be their decision.

'Suppose they won't give you any more time to pay?' Lucy had hesitated.

'You mean suppose they treat me as a debtor and throw me in prison until the estate is sold and the debt paid from the proceeds?' Martin said and she nodded dumbly.

'In that case, you are in charge. If the worst comes to the worst, come to me in London and wait for my release.'

'It could be several months before I see you again.'

Martin clasped her hands in his.

'Lucy, I am relying on you. My mother won't be able to deal with the estate, and Celia and Thomas will only have you to help them. In addition, I expect John Scudamore will be here almost every day asking for confirmation that he has done the right thing. It is a great responsibility, Lucy, but at least you will be here and I know I can trust you.'

After that, how could she say that she

was not sure she could cope with the burden?

Early the next morning, she had packed some food for the start of his journey, and then he had called the family and servants together and told them the news. Mistress Radford, who had come reluctantly, complaining at her morning ritual being disturbed, clutched her handkerchief to her mouth.

'This is my doing!' she said in sudden agony. 'My letters betrayed you and I gave our savings away!'

This was the first time that she had admitted responsibility in any way, and the sudden breakdown shocked them all. Martin went to her and put his arm round her.

'Do not blame yourself, Mother. There were hundreds who knew that I followed King Charles to Worcester, and for all we know our savings are indeed helping to support him in exile.'

Mistress Radford sat up, regaining

her composure, while Lucy digested the information that her mother-in-law must all the while have been feeling some guilt. Martin went off to see John Scudamore.

He returned an hour later with John in anxious attendance and soon his horse was saddled and ready, his scanty luggage in the saddlebags. It was time to say farewell and they stood around a little awkwardly, not knowing what to say. Celia and Thomas, aware that they did not understand all the implications of this sudden departure, kissed him goodbye.

Then Mistress Radford embraced her son, holding him to her tightly.

'God go with you,' she whispered. 'This may be the last time I see you.'

He smiled down at her tenderly.

'I shall be back in a few weeks, Mother, and all will be well. Meanwhile, you know Lucy will look after you.'

Mistress Radford nodded.

'I know we can depend on her.'

This first, public tribute from Mistress Radford took Lucy aback, but Martin had turned to her.

'Goodbye, Lucy. I hope our parting will not be long.'

In front of everyone, she put her arms round his neck and laid her cheek against his. His arms went round her and he held her to him for one long second before he released her and stepped back, smiling.

'Wish me well,' he said, swinging himself up into the saddle, and without more ado turned the horse towards the road that would eventually lead to London.

Lucy watched him till he was out of sight.

Over the next two weeks, the household adjusted to the situation. Mistress Radford resumed her usual occupations and seemed to have forgotten her temporary softening, but Celia and Thomas were so caring and exemplary in behaviour that Lucy found it most unnatural and was relieved when they finally had a quarrel and reverted to normal! As Martin had predicted, John Scudamore often called on her for approval of his actions, and she was careful to always praise him in the hope that his confidence in himself would grow.

At first, scrappy messages came from Martin, dropped off by pedlars and other travellers, always assuring her that his journey was progressing smoothly. Then, as he travelled farther south, the messages stopped.

The days passed uneventfully, but at least Lucy was beginning to think that she could justify Martin's trust that he would come back to find the farms and his family well looked after. Then the weather changed. Crops and stock had been flourishing, but then rain began to fall. Day after day the grey skies lowered miserably. There was no time for anything to recover between downpours and everything seemed to be permanently cold and damp. Crops rotted in the waterlogged fields and weak animals succumbed to disease. Lucy felt as though everything was becoming rotten.

Then she was summoned urgently to the bedside of a local elderly woman. Lucy found her shivering as though cold even while she burned with fever, complaining that her very bones ached. Then another villager fell sick, then another, till every day seemed to bring new cases. It took a long time for sufferers to recover and they seemed so feeble and lacking in vigour for some weeks afterwards.

Lucy and Agnes Lockyer brewed soothing herbal draughts and were kept busy producing the nourishing soups which seemed the only thing the invalids could digest. In some of the village houses there were not enough left healthy to nurse the sick and Lucy was a familiar figure as she went from cottage to cottage organising neighbours to make sure that nobody was left neglected and suffering.

In spite of all she could do, some of

the old and weak died. They were buried in the graveyard next to the old chapel which had not been visited by a minister in over two years. John Scudamore read the burial service over them and Lucy promised that she would get a minister to come and bless the graves later.

Then the fever reached Radford Hall. Master Bateman now spent most of his time sleeping peacefully in his room or nodding by the fire in the kitchen, only rousing himself at dinnertime. He was now too feeble to be entrusted to carry dishes, and limited his duties to telling Maggie what to do, but one morning he did not appear for his morning meal. Agnes Lockyer went to his room and found him feverish and delirious and immediately came in search of Lucy, who hurried back with her to the butler's room.

The old man was tossing restlessly in his bed and when Lucy laid a hand on his forehead it was hot and dry.

'He has the fever,' she said bluntly.

Agnes Lockyer looked down at the bed.

'Is there any hope for him?'

'He is old and was in poor health before this struck him, but we will do our best. Bring me some water and rags to bathe his forehead, and some of that infusion of feverfew.'

Agnes lingered, looking at Master Bateman.

'He came here with the mistress when I was a young girl. He was so tall and imposing that I was terrified of him. Now look at him. Well, it will be the end of an era if he dies.'

With that, she went off to her kitchen to get on with her duties, but word quickly spread of the butler's illness and Lucy, carefully spooning broth into the old man, found Mistress Radford beside her.

'I will take care of him,' the older woman said crisply. 'You can look after the villagers. I hear you have enough work there.'

Lucy stood up, glad to be relieved of

one responsibility.

'There are others I have to see to. When I've finished in the village I'll come back to relieve you.'

'No need,' Mistress Radford said brusquely, picking up the spoon and supporting the old man's head on her arm. 'Master Bateman is my responsibility.'

And indeed she refused to take more than a few brief rests from the task of nursing the old servant over the next two days. Then Lucy was shaken awake by Maggie soon after midnight.

'Mistress Radford asked me to fetch you,' the girl whispered. 'I think Master Bateman is dying.'

Lucy dressed rapidly and went to the sickroom. There, one glance confirmed Maggie's suspicions. Master Bateman was virtually unconscious, sometimes stirring restlessly and mumbling a few unintelligible words.

'Can you do anything for him?' Mistress Radford demanded, but Lucy shook her head.

'I can soothe him a little if we can get him to drink an infusion, but he is too feeble to fight the disease.'

Then she saw how haggard the older woman looked, with dark shadows under her eyes.

'You have been with him without a break for hours. Why don't you go to have a sleep? I'll send for you if there is any change.'

Mistress Radford did not even look up.

'I'll stay with him till the end,' she said bleakly. 'It will not be long now.'

Lucy drew up a chair beside her.

It was a very peaceful end. Towards three o'clock the shallow breathing grew slower, faltered, and stopped. Lucy bent over the frail figure and closed the old man's eyes before turning to where Mistress Radford had sat without moving during their vigil.

'It is over now. Agnes Lockyer and I will prepare him for burial. You must rest.'

Mistress Radford ignored her, gazing

down at the quiet face on the pillow.

'Bateman was already a full-grown man working for my family when I was born. He was with us when the king knighted my father and he knew all about my fantasies of going to court and being a great lady. Such empty dreams! Such a waste of time! Then he came here with me for the happy years with Martin's father. At least he can rest quietly in this valley.'

She stood up slowly, suddenly looking much older.

'I will leave him in your hands now.'

Master Bateman was buried the next day. The Radfords huddled round his grave during the brief ceremony, well wrapped up against the persistent rain. Lucy was conscious of a wind driving their wet clothes against them. Then as they turned to leave she glanced up at the sky and then pointed urgently at the horizon.

'Look!'

The wind was rising so that the clouds were scudding past overhead, and on the horizon, a band of blue was growing wider. As they looked, sunshine filled the far end of the valley.

'The weather has changed at last!' John Scudamore said with deep thankfulness. 'Maybe we can yet save the crops and the stock.'

'And maybe the wind will blow away the fever,' Lucy whispered to herself.

Indeed it did seem that things had changed for the better. Dry, sunny weather seemed to bring better health to everything. Crops given up for lost seemed to reappear magically and the animals were grazing with renewed vigour. Women washed the sweat-stained bedclothes and garments, watched them blow dry, and rejoiced in the fresh, clean smell when they took them in. The convalescent sat in sheltered corners and let the sun warm them and Lucy no longer spent most of her time tending to the sick. For the first time in weeks she was able to sleep peacefully through the night.

But fate had one last blow in store.

Mistress Radford sat at the dinner table one night, upright and dignified as usual, but Lucy noticed that she was eating very little. Then, as she rose to leave the table she suddenly closed her eyes and pitched forward, saving herself from falling by clutching at the edge of the table. Lucy and Maggie hurried to help her sit back in her chair.

'What is the matter? Are you ill?'

'No! I stood up too fast, that is all.'

But when Lucy put her hand on Mistress Radford's forehead it was burning hot.

'You have the fever. Maggie and I will help you to your bed,' she said firmly, and her mother-in-law did not object as the two young women each took her by the arm and helped her slowly to her apartments.

Leaving Maggie to help her into her nightgown, Lucy went to warn Agnes Lockyer that after all they did have one more patient in need of infusions and broth.

Mistress Radford was a strong

woman and at first Lucy was sure that the fever would run its course and then she would make a full recovery. But the illness dragged on and eventually Lucy realised that Mistress Radford was gradually growing weaker.

'I don't understand it,' she said worriedly to Agnes. 'I was sure she would be better by now.'

The cook looked at her sideways.

'Perhaps she doesn't want to get better.'

'What do you mean?'

'She knows that in all probability the estate will be forfeit to Parliament and the Radfords will be penniless and homeless. She also knows that to a certain extent she is to blame for the situation. I think she would rather die than face such a miserable future.'

'She can't die!' Lucy said vehemently. 'I promised Martin I would keep his family safe. I won't let her die!'

Agnes Lockyer chuckled grimly as she stirred one of her pots.

'Mistress Radford was always a

strong-willed woman. You won't stop her doing what she wants to do.'

And in spite of Lucy's tender care and the hours she spent nursing Mistress Radford, finally she had to admit that Agnes was right. Mistress Radford was drifting inexorably away. Lucy hardly left the sickroom during the last days. Mistress Radford drifted in and out of consciousness and when she did speak she was talking to ghosts from the past such as her father and husband. Occasionally she was issuing orders to Master Bateman and Lucy shuddered as she thought of him lying quietly in the graveyard while his mistress spoke to him as if he were alive and young. Once Lucy heard her own name.

'Martin and Lucy think I haven't realised the truth, that they are not really husband and wife,' Mistress Radford was confiding in some invisible listener. 'At first I was glad. I didn't want my grandchild to have a trades-man's blood in his veins, but now I'm not sure. The two of them are well suited and I would like to see my grandson.'

Lucy bent over the sick woman.

'You will, I promise you!'

What did a lie matter so long as it gave Martin's mother the will to live? But the head on the pillow did not respond. The fever was gradually consuming her. Celia and Thomas, as well as Maggie and Agnes Lockyer, joined Lucy by her bedside for the end. She had been silent and motionless for some time, but suddenly she opened her eyes and tried to struggle up.

'William! Wait for me!'

'She's talking to my father,' Celia said shakily.

The dying woman stretched out a feeble hand.

'William! Take my hand. Help me!'

Lucy looked at Mistress Radford, desperately seeking reassurance from her dead love. She took the sick woman's hand in her own warm grasp. Mistress Radford's face relaxed into a contented smile.

'Now I'm safe,' she said, and closed her eyes for the last time.

Celia burst into tears and Thomas looked uncertainly round as Maggie threw her apron over her face and started to sob.

'Take them away, Agnes,' Lucy said softly and the cook ushered them out, leaving Lucy alone with Mistress Radford.

'I promise you I will take care of Celia,' she told the silent face, 'and I will care for Martin, too, as much as he will let me.'

But what use were her promises? She had told Martin that she would look after his family, but now his mother was dead.

10

Everybody from the village who was able came to Mistress Radford's burial, aware that they were saying goodbye to that past golden era when the king had sat securely on his throne and the prospering Radfords had expected to stay in their valley for centuries to come. John Scudamore was overcome at the prospect of officiating and begged Lucy to choose someone else.

'No, John,' she said firmly. 'Mistress Radford knew you for many years and I know she respected you. In the absence of her son, I am sure she would want you to say the words of the funeral office over her grave.'

Reassured, he spoke clearly and reverently before the audience of his own people, knowing they shared his feelings at this moment. While Lucy stood with her arms round her at the graveside, Celia wept for the mother who had rarely shown affection to her late-born daughter. Agnes Lockyer and Maggie were also in tears, like many of the other listeners. Afterwards, the villagers called at Radford Hall to murmur their condolences to Lucy and Celia while Agnes and Maggie busied themselves supplying food and drink.

Lucy had not cried. She had felt nothing since that moment when she had said farewell to her mother-in-law. Now she thanked the villagers and encouraged them to help themselves to the refreshments.

That evening's dinner was a gloomy affair. Celia looked round the table tearfully.

'A few weeks ago, we had Master Bateman, Martin and my mother. Now there are just the three of us.'

'Martin will come back,' Thomas said hurriedly, turning to Lucy. 'He will, won't he?'

'I hope so, Thomas, but I don't know.'

'What happens to us if he doesn't?' Celia said with a touch of hysteria.

'Then we go to him. Whatever happens, we will be together.'

She spoke more sharply than she meant to and they felt reprimanded rather than comforted, she knew, but she hadn't the energy necessary to reassure them and the meal ended in doleful silence.

Nightmares made Lucy's sleep restless that night. She ran down endless corridors, searching for Martin but never finding him. She woke late, still tired, and dressed hurriedly. For the first time in many days she had the time to turn to her mirror to check her appearance before she left the room. She stopped suddenly and peered at her reflection. A pale, thin face looked back at her with dark circles under its eyes. The fair hair had lost its lustre. She looked much older than her years and had lost weight. It was the first time since the fever had struck the village that she realised how much energy it had cost her to look after the villagers, both sick and well. She felt she had said farewell to her youth.

Listlessly, she trailed down the stairs to the dining-room where Maggie told her that both Celia and Thomas had breakfasted early and gone out.

'Tell Mistress Lockyer I'll come and see her as soon as I have eaten,' Lucy said. 'Then I will get on with work.'

Maggie hovered at the door.

'What is there for you to do, Mistress Radford?'

Before, she had always said Mistress Lucy, but now Lucy was undisputed mistress of the house.

'There are my mother-in-law's rooms to be cleared and tidied for a start, and it is a long time since this table saw any beeswax.'

'Do you have to do it today?' Maggie asked boldly. 'Agnes and I were saying that it was time you had a rest. It's a lovely day. Why don't you go for a walk this morning?'

Lucy realised that it was true that for

the first time in many weeks there were no urgent tasks waiting for her. There were no invalids waiting for her attention. Did it matter if the table went unpolished for another day? What was the point of reorganising Mistress Radford's apartments when a new owner with different ideas might soon take over the house?

She looked out the window and saw blue sky above the hills. Today would be her holiday. Wearing stout shoes and with a cloak wrapped round her against the fresh breeze, she set out by herself and walked steadily along, gradually getting higher and higher until she could sit down on the grass and look at the valley spread out before her. In the bright clear light she could see the villagers' houses, the chapel and Radford Hall.

She had found work which suited her here and as she had taken her place in the community the valley had become home to her. But if she had to leave she knew that there was a wide world beyond the valley. She would be sad to leave Radford Hall, but not afraid.

She jumped resolutely to her feet and set off back down the track. The walk in the summer air had refreshed her and she had enjoyed the luxury of being alone with no-one making demands on her. As Lucy came down the slopes she lost her view of the village. Her path took her past the chapel and as she came out from behind the building she saw a man standing by Mistress Radford's fresh grave. She wondered who the lonely mourner was, but a second glance made her breath leave her in a harsh gasp. She gathered up her skirts and ran towards him.

'Martin!'

He swung round at the sound of her voice, but she stopped abruptly a few feet away from him.

'I'm sorry I failed you, Martin. I tried to save her but she wanted to die.'

She did not hear what he said in reply because everything seemed to become very vague and the world seemed to be spinning round her.

'But I never faint!' she said indignantly as she crumpled to the ground.

When Lucy regained consciousness, she felt very weak and tired and it took an effort to lift her heavy eyelids and turn her head to one side. At the same time as she realised that she was in her own bed, there was a rustle of skirts and Celia was bending over her, her face bright with relief.

'You're awake at last! I'll tell Martin.'

There was the swift tap of her shoes on the floor, then the sound of the door opening and closing. Lucy sank back into a light doze and when she woke again Martin himself was sitting by the bedside.

'Have I got the fever?' she said huskily and he shook his head before lifting her shoulders gently so that she could have a drink of water.

'No. You were simply exhausted and in desperate need of sleep.'

She lay back on the pillows, her eyes on his face. There were grim lines on his face as if the past weeks had not been easy. She longed to interrogate him about what had happened in London but lacked the energy to put the words together. He smiled suddenly as he saw her anxious face.

'Don't worry. I have come home with good news. The Radfords are staying at Radford Hall.'

She sighed with relief, but before he could say more Celia had hurried into the room.

'Mistress Lockyer wants to know if Lucy is awake and does she want anything to eat? And two more of the villagers are here asking how she is.'

'What happened?' Lucy managed. 'Did I faint?'

Celia giggled.

'You fainted, then half the village saw Martin carrying you back to the Hall, and since then you've been sound asleep. It is nearly noon. You have almost slept the clock round twice.'

Lucy struggled to her elbows.

'I must get up.'

'Why?' Martin demanded. 'If you need more rest you can stay in bed. How do you feel?'

She considered.

'Hungry,' she said with surprise, and he laughed happily.

'That is a good sign. I'll tell Agnes Lockyer to bring you some food, and then I can tell the latest callers that you have recovered. I think all the village has been here in the last few hours asking how you were.'

Agnes Lockyer brought her a tray of food. She told Lucy that Martin had returned soon after Lucy had set out on her walk.

'So I had to tell him about his mother and the other poor souls,' she said. 'When he found you were not in the house he was anxious to know you were safe and then he went to visit his mother's grave.'

Finally Lucy asked to be left alone. She got up and washed and dressed slowly, putting on the blue dress she had made for herself, and arranged her hair carefully. When she looked in the mirror she was glad to see that the long rest seemed to have improved her appearance a little. Then she made her way down the main staircase, holding on to the oak rail. Before she had reached the last flight, Martin had appeared in the hall. He took her arm and led her into the drawing-room and settled her in a comfortable chair.

'Would you like anything? A glass of wine?' he suggested, but when she refused he took his own seat opposite her.

At first they spoke of his mother's death.

'Agnes Lockyer told me what happened,' Martin said soberly. 'And she told me that you helped my mother to die happy.'

There was a pause, and then Lucy roused herself.

'Now I want to hear what happened in London.'

He shifted a little uneasily, avoiding her gaze.

'I've been trying to think how I would tell you ever since I left London,' he began. 'But the story is not what you are expecting, and some of it will distress you.'

'So tell me from the beginning.'

He fell silent until she stirred impatiently and then he began abruptly, gazing at a point above her head.

'As soon as I reached London and had found an inn where I could lodge, I went to the commissioners' office and there I met once again the gentleman who had known your father. I started to explain how so far I had only gathered part of the fine but he stopped me and said that was not why he had asked me to come to London.'

Lucy's eyes widened in astonishment and she waited for him to continue.

'He told me how surprised he had been to hear from you that your father had lost all his money, and when he went back he caused investigations to be made. With his authority, it did not take long to find out the truth. Your father had taken risks, but they had proved worthwhile. One project in particular made handsome profits. Your father died a rich man.'

'But Walter Thomson wrote to me saying that my father was virtually penniless!'

Martin looked at her briefly.

'Your father and Master Thomson had rooms in the same lodging house. The day before your father died, he was heard having a furious quarrel with Master Thomson. He accused him of forging his signature in order to obtain some money and dismissed him from his service. The next morning Walter Thomson came rushing downstairs and told the landlord that he had gone to your father's room to plead with him to forgive him this one episode because of his previous good service and had found your father dead. Soon afterwards Master Thomson had somehow gained enough capital to set up in business on his own account and prospered quite amazingly. The commissioner discovered that in fact Thomson had forged a number of documents that gave him control of your father's money.'

Lucy said nothing, but her face was white.

'After a year had passed, Thomson must have thought his crimes would never be discovered, and he must have been horrified when he found his affairs were being investigated. He bribed a clerk to tell him what had happened and found that the commissioner had spoken to you here. That was when he hurried up here, hoping that he could get you to sign a document that would appear to authorise his control of the money and stop further questioning. But you did not sign it and meanwhile his forgeries had been discovered. When he returned to London he was arrested.'

He leaned forward.

'Lucy, I am desperately sorry to have to tell you this. I saw you with him and

I know you cared for the man.'

She shook her head.

'I told you that he was part of my youth, a reminder of my life with my father. He meant nothing to me as a man.'

'If that is indeed so, then I must tell you that stealing the money was not all he was guilty of. Your father showed no sign of ill health before that quarrel. The commissioner thought the coincidence of your father's death was too convenient to be true and after questioning, Thomson confessed that he murdered your father, smothered him in his bed before it could become generally known that Walter Thomson had tried to steal from your father.'

She gave a harsh sob of shock and had to struggle to control herself.

'But my father was a good man! He treated Walter well.'

'The man was greedy for your father's wealth and when he saw a way to get it the temptation was too great.'

She brooded for a while, Martin

watching her carefully.

'What happens now?'

'By now he will have paid the penalty for murder. The commissioner had summoned me to tell me what had been discovered, and to entrust me, as your husband, with the money that had been recovered.'

'And the other affair? The fine?'

'He had already deducted that from your father's money.'

Her body rose with a deep sigh.

'So at least Radford Hall and the valley are safe! Life can go on as before.'

'No!' he said suddenly, starting up and beginning to stride about the room. 'You don't understand, Lucy. Remember your father's will? He left a third of his fortune to you and the rest to Thomas. You are both wealthy.'

'And you are my husband, so my money is yours.'

'I am your husband in name only. With the money you can have this mockery of a marriage dissolved. You and Thomas will be free to leave here and start a new life in London or back in Worcester, or anywhere you like.'

She stared at him.

'And is this what you want?'

But there was no need for an answer. Martin had married her reluctantly to save his life but had not wanted the Puritan daughter of a merchant as a wife. She and Thomas had just been another burden to bear. But if she did as he said, Martin would also be free. Henrietta Downing might be betrothed to another man, but there were plenty of other ladies of his own kind who would be glad to marry him, especially when it became known that there was no longer any threat to his possession of his estate.

She loved him, but to make him happy she would have to leave him, leave the place that had become her home, and give him his freedom.

'How would I go about the matter?' she asked him dully and he shrugged.

'It would be a matter for the lawyers.'

'Then I suppose it is the sensible thing to do.'

He nodded. There seemed nothing left for them to say. She stood up slowly.

'I must go and speak to Agnes Lockyer.'

She walked to the door and then looked back. Martin had slumped down in his chair. Suddenly she was filled with anger. Why should she give up the man she loved so easily? She hurried back to confront him.

'You haven't answered my question,' she challenged him. 'Is this what you want?'

He looked up at her.

'Isn't it what you want? You wanted security for Thomas and yourself, not me as a husband. I've given you a roof over your head, and food to eat, but in return you have had to work like a servant and I have heard from Agnes Lockyer how many hours you have spent recently caring for the sick. Now you can have a life of comfort and leisure. That must be what you want.'

She stood before him, hands on her hips, anger giving her the courage to speak.

'That is by no means what I want. I want to stay here at Radford Hall with you, as your true wife. I want to bear your children and watch them grow up in this valley, which is my home now as much as yours.'

He stared at her in wonder.

'Why should you want to do that?'

'Because I love you, Martin Radford.'

There was an instant of pure stillness and then he was up and holding her arms so tightly that they hurt.

'You love me?'

'Yes,' she said, tears coming to her eyes.

She had made a complete fool of herself. How could she look him in the face again? But then she found herself in his arms, and he was kissing her. It was the first time a man had ever kissed her with passion and she responded awkwardly at first, and then with eagerness, and it was some time before he lifted his head and looked down at her.

'Lucy, I realised I loved you months ago. Have you any idea what it has been like to share a bed with you, want you, and not be able to touch you?'

'Yes! I know as well as you do!' she said fiercely. 'So why were you trying to send me away?'

'Because I thought you would be happier.'

'And I was going to let you do it!'

She drew his face down to hers again.

'They're kissing!' Thomas said in some disgust from the doorway, and Lucy and Martin broke apart.

'John Scudamore is here again. He says some slates have come off the old barn's roof and he wants to know what to do,' Thomas told them as he entered the room.

Martin looked anxious.

'That barn's about ready to collapse,' he said to Lucy when Thomas had gone. 'We'll have to see what we can do to repair it.'

'Nonsense!' Lucy said. 'Remember, we are a wealthy family now. Let's tell him we will build a new one. We'll have the stables redone at the same time and there are many things I long to have done to the house.'

Martin laughed, but stopped quickly. 'Are you sure?'

She smiled at him and slipped her arm through his.

'Quite sure, dear husband. This is the home that we love and you are the man I love. Here we will stay, as one happy family, for all time.'

THE END

We do hope that you have enjoyed reading this large print book.

Did you know that all of our titles are available for purchase?

We publish a wide range of high quality large print books including:
Romances, Mysteries, Classics
General Fiction
Non Fiction and Westerns

Special interest titles available in large print are:
The Little Oxford Dictionary
Music Book, Song Book
Hymn Book, Service Book

Also available from us courtesy of Oxford University Press:
Young Readers' Dictionary
(large print edition)
Young Readers' Thesaurus
(large print edition)

For further information or a free brochure, please contact us at:
Ulverscroft Large Print Books Ltd.,
The Green, Bradgate Road, Anstey,
Leicester, LE7 7FU, England.
Tel: (00 44) **0116 236 4325**
Fax: (00 44) **0116 234 0205**

Joanna Baxter flies from Sydney to run her parents' small farm in the Adelaide Hills while they recover from a road accident. But after crossing swords with Riley Kemp, life is anything but uneventful. Gradually she discovers that Riley's passionate nature and quirky sense of humour are capturing her emotions, but a magical day spent with him on the coast comes to an abrupt end when the elegant Greta intervenes. Did Riley love Greta after all?

SUMMER IN HANOVER SQUARE

Charlotte Grey

The impoverished Margaret Lambart is suddenly flung into all the glitter of the Season in Regency London. Suspected by her godmother's nephew, the influential Marquis St. George, of being merely a common adventuress, she has, nevertheless, a brilliant success, and attracts the attentions of the young Duke of Oxford. However, when the Marquis discovers that Margaret is far from wanting a husband he finds he has to revise his estimate of her true worth.

CONFLICT OF HEARTS

Gillian Kaye

Somerset, at the end of World War I: Daniel Holley, unhappily married to an ailing wife and father of four grown-up children, is attracted to beautiful schoolteacher Harriet Bray, but he knows his love is hopeless. Daniel's only daughter, Amy, who dreams of becoming a milliner and is caught up in her love for young bank clerk John Tottle, looks on as the drama of Daniel and Harriet's fate and happiness gradually unfolds.

THE SOLDIER'S WOMAN

Freda M. Long

When Lieutenant Alain d'Albert was deserted by his girlfriend, a replacement was at hand in the shape of Christina Calvi, whose yearning for respectability through marriage did not quite coincide with her profession as a soldier's woman. Christina's obsessive love for Alain was not returned. The handsome hussar married an heiress and banished the soldier's woman from his life. But Christina was unswerving in the pursuit of her dream and Alain found his resistance weakening . . .